RESULT

GAINED XP: LEVEL INCREASED BY 1.

GAINED XP: LEVEL INCREASED BY 1.

GAINED XP: LEVEL INCREASED BY 1.

DUNGEON TAKEDOWN REWARD: LEVEL INCREASED BY 20.

BONUS REWARD: LEVEL INCREASED BY 50.

Only I'm allowed to level up this way. I *will* become the best in the world... and I'll get there the fastest."

AMANE RIN

AWAKENED TO THE UNIQUE SKILL "DUNGEON TELEPORTATION," HE IS THE ONLY ADVENTURER IN THE WORLD TO WHOM THE RULES DO NOT APPLY.

THE WORLD'S FASTEST LEVEL UP

With strength that was impossible only one week ago, Rin charges into an evenly matched battle against an orc general. Rei watches on with her hands clasped together and prays for his success.

"Go win... Rin."

"I want to talk to him again. Strange that I feel this way. We've only just met."

KUROSAKI REI

A TALENTED ADVENTURER WHO SURPASSED LEVEL 500 THREE MONTHS AGO. SHE POSSESSES A UNIQUE SKILL CALLED "MAGIC SWORD." SHE PROJECTS A STOIC PERSONALITY, BUT SHE FEELS STRONGLY FOR HER FRIENDS.

"Can I ask for your number?"

KASAI YUI

A NOVICE ADVENTURER WHOSE LIFE RIN SAVED INSIDE A DUNGEON. THOUGH SWEET AND SLIGHTLY AIRHEADED, SHE IS AN EXTREMELY RARE HEALER.

With strength that was impossible only one week ago, Rin charges into an evenly matched battle against an orc general. Rei watches on with her hands clasped together and prays for his success.

"Go win... Rin."

"I want to talk to him again. Strange that I feel this way. We've only just met."

KUROSAKI REI

A TALENTED ADVENTURER WHO SURPASSED LEVEL 500 THREE MONTHS AGO. SHE POSSESSES A UNIQUE SKILL CALLED "MAGIC SWORD." SHE PROJECTS A STOIC PERSONALITY, BUT SHE FEELS STRONGLY FOR HER FRIENDS.

"Can I ask for your number?"

KASAI YUI

A NOVICE ADVENTURER WHOSE LIFE RIN SAVED INSIDE A DUNGEON. THOUGH SWEET AND SLIGHTLY AIRHEADED, SHE IS AN EXTREMELY RARE HEALER.

THE WORLD'S FASTEST LEVEL↑UP

SEKAI SAISOKU NO LEVEL UP Vol. 1
©Nagato Yamata, fame 2021
First published in Japan in 2021 by
KADOKAWA CORPORATION, Tokyo.
English translation rights arranged with
KADOKAWA CORPORATION, Tokyo.

Seven Seas press and purchase enquiries can be sent to
Marketing Manager Lianne Sentar at press@gomanga.com.
Information regarding the distribution and purchase of
digital editions is available from Digital Manager CK Russell
at digital@gomanga.com.

Follow Seven Seas Entertainment online at
sevenseasentertainment.com.

TRANSLATION: Morgan Watchorn
ADAPTATION: Nikita Greene
COVER DESIGN: Nicky Lim
LOGO DESIGN: George Panella
INTERIOR LAYOUT & DESIGN: Clay Gardner
COPY EDITOR: Meg van Huygen
PROOFREADER: Cheri Ebisu
LIGHT NOVEL EDITOR: Mercedez Clewis
PREPRESS TECHNICIAN: Melanie Ujimori, Jules Valera
PRODUCTION MANAGER: Lissa Pattillo
EDITOR-IN-CHIEF: Julie Davis
ASSOCIATE PUBLISHER: Adam Arnold
PUBLISHER: Jason DeAngelis

ISBN: 978-1-63858-635-7
Printed in Canada
First Printing: January 2023
10 9 8 7 6 5 4 3 2 1

THE WORLD'S FASTEST LEVEL UP

NOVEL 1

WRITTEN BY
NAGATO YAMATA

ILLUSTRATED BY
fame

Airship

Seven Seas Entertainment

THE WORLD'S FASTEST LEVEL UP

CONTENTS

PROLOGUE

TWENTY YEARS AGO, underground labyrinths called dungeons spawned all around the world.

In those dungeons existed monsters: creatures beyond the scope of human imagination. Modern weaponry couldn't hold a candle to their strength and power. With them came magic stones—a usable energy source far better than fossil fuels—and countless more otherworldly things that didn't operate under the known rules of physics. Most remarkable and wondrous of them all was the concept of the level system.

Levels.

Stats.

Skills.

Those once existed only in the world of video games and anime, but now, they were *real*. Subduing monsters granted experience points that increased levels. Increased levels led to boosted stats: fulfilling certain requirements allowed a person to gain supernatural powers called skills. This led to the advent of adventurers, people who used their powers to overcome monsters while gathering magic stones and other dungeon resources to sell.

The power of adventurers was tremendous. One adventurer could rival the military strength of an entire nation. That was why adventurers gained such high social status. A globally-ranked adventurer had more wealth, prestige, and privileges than any politician or celebrity could ever obtain. Many people dreamed of becoming adventurers of that caliber.

Unfortunately, not everyone's dreams could come true.

Two huge obstacles stood in the way. First, the level system didn't work equally for everyone. Only a fraction of people could obtain stats. As for the second condition... Well, because of the way dungeons worked, adventurers who arrived late to the party were at a severe disadvantage. Yet even with those obstacles, people still tried to become adventurers. They spent their days dungeon diving in hopes of getting rich quick.

But I, Amane Rin, wanted to become an adventurer for a completely different reason.

You see, years ago, when my sister and I were out together, we were involved in an incident where monsters that should only be inside a dungeon escaped onto the surface. A monster larger than the both of us approached, and I truly thought we were going to die. But at that exact moment, an adventurer slew the monster and saved our lives.

I could never get the image of his back—and his overwhelming strength—out of my mind. From that moment on, I wanted to become just like him.

Time passed, and the memory grew fuzzy. I didn't know who the man was. However, that warmth I felt in my chest remained clear as day. I wanted to become as strong as he was so I could protect the people I loved.

I graduated high school, passed my adventurer qualifications, and successfully got my stats, but that didn't satisfy me. To become an acting adventurer, I needed to meet another condition: getting a skill. After all, an adventurer's innate talent was determined by the skills they gained upon obtaining their stats.

For example, a sword skill would make someone a knight; a magical skill would make someone a sorcerer. Now, if someone didn't gain a skill upon obtaining their stats, there *were* other ways to get skills. That being said, a skill that emerged right away showed the level system acknowledged the person's talent. Most people who received a skill early outperformed people who gained the same skill later. If someone didn't gain a skill alongside their stats, their adventurer career was basically doomed.

I gained two skills.

The first was Enhanced Strength. Anyone with this skill possessed only the bare minimum talent for physical movement. It pretty much meant that the adventurer was average in their ability to fight: nothing to write home about. That wasn't great, but my second skill was the real deal. Somehow, I got a skill that no one else had. My unique skill: Dungeon Teleportation. Like the name said, it gave me the rule-defying ability to freely move my location within a dungeon.

Damn, did people envy me for it—but only at first. With Dungeon Teleportation LV 1, I could only move a maximum of five meters at a rate of ten seconds per meter. On top of that, I could only teleport myself. Raising my skill level barely moved the needle. Soon, other adventurers started to think of it as a useless skill, and they stopped inviting me to join their parties.

Unfortunately, when it came to dungeon diving, forming parties was vital. Forget success as a great adventurer: basic dungeon diving was hard as hell alone. I didn't give up, though. My goal to become strong, like the adventurer who saved me that day, never wavered. Besides, a gut feeling told me that my Dungeon Teleportation skill wasn't the useless ability people assumed. I wanted to prove them wrong, so I kept training and dungeon diving.

One year after my very first dungeon, the day finally came— Dungeon Teleportation *awakened*.

CHAPTER 1

AWAKENING DUNGEON TELEPORTATION

YUNAGI DUNGEON, Classification: D-rank, floor fifteen. That was where I took on three goblins at once.

"Haaa!"

I whipped my short sword over my head. The tip caught one goblin's throat and ripped it wide open. From the corner of my eye, I saw it choke on its own blood and collapse as I went after the other two. They ran at me with a combo attack, but—

"Too slow!!!" I shouted.

The goblins that spawned in Yunagi Dungeon were level 120; I was level 194. Sure, numbers mattered, but the massive difference in our levels squashed any advantage. I lightly parried each goblin's club and struck back with two strong swipes of my short sword. They both collapsed with a bloody gargle.

"Subjugation complete," I said to myself. At the same time, the familiar sound of the level system dinged in my brain.

"Gained XP. Level increased by 1!"

"Sweet! Here it comes. Stats, open!"

At my command, the stats screen appeared in front of me.

AMANE RIN

LEVEL: 195

SP: 300

HP: 1,600/1,600

MP: 350/350

ATTACK: 390

DEFENSE: 290

SPEED: 400

INTELLIGENCE: 290

RESISTANCE: 290

LUCK: 290

SKILLS: Dungeon Teleportation LV 9, Enhanced Strength LV 3

DUNGEON TELEPORTATION LV 9

REQUIRED MP: 3 MP × distance (meters)

CONDITIONS: Teleportation can only occur inside the current dungeon.

TELEPORTATION DISTANCE: Maximum 20 meters.

ACTIVATION TIME: 2 seconds × distance (meters)

SCOPE: User and user's belongings.

Like the system sound indicated, my level grew from 194 to 195. My stats increased a bit too. Unfortunately, a look at my stats did nothing but depress me.

"My level is increasing nicely, but that doesn't change the fact I could still end up a bottom-of-the-barrel adventurer. The top-ranked adventurers in the world surpass 100,000. Compared to them, I've got a long way to go."

It had been twenty years since dungeons first appeared in our world. The front-runners had a huge head start. Considering I only had a year of experience, maybe it was presumptuous of me to try to catch up to them.

Oh, yeah. I think Yunagi Dungeon's level-up reward is five levels, I recalled.

That was crucial information. The lowest floor of every dungeon possessed a boss room where the dungeon boss lurked. Defeating the boss and taking down the whole dungeon offered all kinds of rewards. The total rewards varied with each dungeon, but every dungeon had a level-up reward. We adventurers could level up according to the figures set by the specific dungeon, regardless of our individual experience.

E-rank dungeons gave one level, A-rank dungeons gave a hundred levels, and so on. The number depended on the dungeon's difficulty. In this case, Yunagi Dungeon—a D-rank dungeon—rewarded five levels.

Back when people were first figuring out the dungeons, there was a theory that defeating the dungeon itself over and over to gain levels would be faster than defeating monsters. But that theory died soon after it was formed.

Why? Because there was something that made it impossible.

After an adventurer defeated a dungeon, they had to deal with a Span—a week-long waiting period before they could try again. No one knew what caused the Span to exist but based on the information adventurers had gathered from around the world, all dungeons were linked together. That link meant we couldn't storm a different dungeon to get around the Span. That was why adventurers who arrived late to the game were basically screwed.

"I still can't wrap my head around this absurd setup..."

I mean, I'd spent the last year fighting monsters ranked higher than me, but the people who spent the last five years safely beating lower-ranked dungeons were higher level than I was! How unfair was *that*?

Not to mention, when it came to a full party, the dungeon gave level-up rewards to everyone, no matter how many assisted. If five people took down Yunagi Dungeon, they'd each gain five levels. It was completely separate from the experience points—XP—split among a party killing monsters together. That was why most adventurers partied up with people close to their skill level and undertook whatever dungeons would give them level-up rewards. Everyone did it that way, but it was so *frustrating*!

I admit, I understood why no one wanted to form a party with me.

"Well, it's not against the rules to go solo."

I didn't need other people to close the level gap. I just needed to center my actions around exterminating monsters. Sadly, that strategy meant I had to dungeon dive every day, which was the least time-effective method. Despite knowing the disadvantages and obstacles, I still soloed and adventured without defeating dungeons.

Little did I know, my circumstances were about to radically change.

"If I get the level-up reward for this dungeon, I can jump straight to level 200."

I'd waited for this moment since I became an adventurer. With our level system, every ten levels, an adventurer gained 100 skill points, or SP. SP was the fuel needed to strengthen skills. At that moment, I had 300 SP. Defeating Yunagi Dungeon would give me 100, boosting my total SP pool to 400. That was exactly the number of points I needed to raise Dungeon Teleportation from LV 9 to LV 10.

It varied by the skill, but plenty of skills gained a massive strength boost when they jumped to LV 10. I wanted to test it out immediately.

"Okay, I'm gonna lose out on a week of dungeon diving for cash but cracking eggs and making omelets and all that. Here goes nothing!"

With my mind made up, I traveled down to the twentieth floor of Yunagi Dungeon. That marked the bottom floor, where the boss awaited: a level 150 twin-tailed beast. With its agile dual-tail attacks, it was a tough monster to get a grip on. But this was my third time encountering it, and we had a big difference in levels now. I stayed calm and overwhelmed it.

Once it was dead, the system dinged in my mind.

"Dungeon Takedown Reward: Level increased by 5!"

AMANE RIN		
LEVEL: 200	**SP:** 400	
HP: 1,640/1,640	**MP:** 360/360	
ATTACK: 400	**DEFENSE:** 300	**SPEED:** 410
INTELLIGENCE: 300	**RESISTANCE:** 300	**LUCK:** 290

SKILL: Dungeon Teleportation LV 9, Enhanced Strength LV 3

"Whew."

I paused to take a breath.

Today, in this very moment, my life as an adventurer could change dramatically, I thought.

"So much happened this past year."

After I graduated high school, I passed my adventurer's qualifications and gained my unique skill, Dungeon Teleportation. People were shocked, at first, by the ability to defy the laws of physics and freely move within a dungeon. I had high expectations on my shoulders. But in practice, my skill carried many weaknesses. People started to write it off as a useless ability.

Damn, that memory *really* irritated me.

I kept stubborn faith in my skill, though: my desire to become as strong as the man I met that fateful day never disappeared. That was why, while the other adventurers who started around the same time as me leveled up, I poured my blood, sweat, and tears into leveling up even *more*. Now was the time to see if it was all worth it.

"Here we go."

With my mind made up, I applied every last one of my skill points to Dungeon Teleportation.

Which part would change? Teleportation distance? Activation time? Scope? Or—

"Dungeon Teleportation skill LV 10."

"Skill conditions have changed."

"Teleportation can only occur inside the current dungeon. →
Teleportation can only occur in dungeons that have already been visited."

The system stopped sounding inside my head.

"Teleportation can only occur in dungeons that have already been visited...?"

It took a while for the meaning to sink in. Eventually, I understood that this wasn't the result I hoped for.

"I should've known... Figures life wouldn't be that easy."

Not, *Teleportation can occur anywhere in the dungeon.*

Not, *Activation time is reduced to X seconds.*

Not, *Scope includes other adventurers.*

I'd imagined a variety of different outcomes, but none of them sucked quite as much as this one.

Well, not that I fully understood what this one *meant*. Even if I could teleport to dungeons I'd been to, at a minimum, they were separated by a whole kilometer. If I tried to ramp up my skill level to teleport even twenty meters, it would take so long I'd never actually get to put it into practice.

This change was completely pointless.

I let out a huge, disappointed sigh. One year of hoping and trying, crushed in a second. Nobody could blame me for being upset.

While I wallowed in my sorrows, a soft light enveloped my body, a signal that the dungeon's teleportation spell was going to activate and teleport me outside.

"*Ugh*...I'd better hurry."

I collected the magic stones from the twin-tailed beast's corpse in a rush. These stones always existed inside monster bodies, and I never passed up the chance to gather them. Since they were such an excellent energy source, I could sell them for a high price. Besides, the dungeon would automatically absorb and destroy whatever I didn't collect in time, so it was a waste to leave them. Man, when I stopped to think about it, dungeons were strange places.

Once I had my magic stones, I silently waited for the teleportation spell to activate. Truth was, I was so upset, I wanted to cry into my pillow for three days and three nights straight. But I still tried to think ahead, knowing I couldn't sulk forever.

"The next time my skill can evolve in a significant way is at level 20. Who knows how many years that'll take, but all I can do is try again."

I slapped my cheeks with both hands to reenergize myself. At the same time, the teleportation spell activated.

"Guess I'll go home..."

I carried my disappointment with me like a stone and left Yunagi Dungeon behind. But one hour later, I would learn something more.

The *true* value of Dungeon Teleportation.

Once I sold my dungeon spoils, I boarded the train and rode to the station nearest to my house. It didn't take long to defeat Yunagi Dungeon, so the sun still hung high in the sky.

On the walk home, I paused in a familiar place. Shion Park was the largest park in town. Without thinking, I expected to see kids playing catch or something, but I didn't. Instead, I saw adventurers with their weapons.

Three years ago, an E-rank dungeon called Shion Dungeon appeared in the park bearing the same name. Those adventurers probably came to defeat it. Lots of adventurers were restless to keep working, or maybe they didn't have much experience.

"I think this was the first dungeon I faced. It's a good one for beginners," I mused to myself.

Not a lot to loot, though. Weak monsters meant low experience points, and the level-up reward only granted one level. Any adventurer remotely worth their salt wouldn't think it was worth challenging. Even I only went down there a handful of times.

"Might as well check it out."

I had time to kill, so I walked into the park. I didn't plan to attempt it. Not that I could, anyway, since I had my week-long Span hanging over my head. I was just feeling nostalgic.

When I approached the entrance, the dungeon supervisor turned and held a small machine out at me. "Scan your Adventurer Card, please."

"Sure."

I extended my driver's license-sized Adventurer Card. The machine beeped.

Like the name implied, an Adventurer Card was given to those who obtained their adventurer qualifications. It recorded the adventurer's name, age, the ranks of the dungeons they had faced, and a few other pieces of demographic information.

Dungeon entrance times and exit times were also recorded by the card. Having one was mandatory to enter a dungeon.

Naturally, someone needed to account for adventurers in the event they were involved in an accident inside a dungeon and couldn't make it back. Hence the existence of dungeon supervisors. They were sent by a government-affiliated organization called the Dungeon Association. Besides recording the foot traffic, they offered other kinds of support to adventurers too.

"Thank you for your cooperation. Take care!" the supervisor said.

I accepted the supervisor's words in silence and stepped toward the tip of a tower that jutted from the ground. Once I reached the entrance built into its side, I passed through and descended the stairs into the large rectangular space underground.

This space was called the Return Zone. Technically, it wasn't part of the dungeon, so Dungeon Teleportation didn't work here. All dungeons had a Return Zone with a singular purpose. Once the adventurer defeated the dungeon, the teleportation spell dropped them here. Yunagi Dungeon's was identical to every dungeon in the world.

"Well, that's not that important."

I ignored my surroundings and headed straight toward the Gate, a passage that must be crossed in order to enter the dungeon. Past there lay the dungeon's true beginning. I followed the familiar path toward the Gate and tried to enter, but an invisible power pushed me back. I couldn't get in.

"Figures."

Gates could repulse people who were too low-level to take it on, but an E-rank dungeon like Shion Dungeon didn't have that. Anyone could enter it, even people without adventurer qualifications. However, I couldn't enter the Gate because of the Span.

"Ugh. If it weren't for the Span, I could grind these dungeons like they're nothing and level up at warp speed..."

I was hardly the first adventurer to think so. Some adventurers attempted to destroy the walls next to the Gate, but no matter how strong a spell they blasted, they couldn't make a scratch. There was no cheating the Span.

Then, a wild thought struck me. *Hey, what if Dungeon Teleportation could get me inside?*

Leveling up changed the condition of my skill from movement within the current dungeon to any dungeon I'd ever been in. If I couldn't pass through the Gate, could I still get inside?

"Nah, I doubt it'll work...but trying never hurt anybody."

At least there was no one around to judge me if it didn't work. I attempted to use Dungeon Teleportation. In my mind, I visualized a spot beyond the Gate to Shion Dungeon. A distance of one meter inside. Activation time: two seconds per meter. I had no hope that this would work, but I waited for the time to pass.

And then—

"No. Freaking. Way...!"

My eyes went wide with shock. I mean, how could they not? The inside of Shion Dungeon was right in front of me.

"It worked?! It really worked!!!"

I was so sure it wouldn't, but I stood in the proof. Shock and elation warred in my chest and developed into a feeling I could not describe. Could I strategize without needing to worry about the Span anymore? If that was possible, that meant I could level up much more effectively than before!

"Wait. I need to get a grip. Getting inside is one thing, but that means nothing if I can't obtain level-up rewards."

It was too soon to think I'd beaten the system. I took several deep breaths and forced myself to settle down. "Okay. Onward."

Once I got myself together, I headed for the bottom floor. Since Shion Dungeon was easy enough for anyone to solo at level 10, I beat the whole thing within the hour. Then, the moment of triumph came: I successfully gained the level-up rewards.

"Ha ha ha...I did it! *I did it!*" This time, my restraint went out the window. I shouted my joy full force.

This would be a serious game changer.

Thanks to Dungeon Teleportation, I might be the only person in the world with no restrictions on level-up rewards! Even grinding the same E-rank and D-rank dungeons would do the trick. Heck, I could grow my level *way* more easily than facing the powerful monsters found in A-rank dungeons!

"Yes! Now that I know the drill..."

After that, I tackled Shion Dungeon over and over with an enormous grin on my face. In the time it took for dusk to fall, I grew nine levels.

◆ ⌃ ◆

Unlimited leveling up was so fun, I lost track of time. When I left the dungeon, the sun had set completely, so I hurried home.

"I-I'm home," I said, cautiously opening the door.

"You're late, oniichan!"

"Whoa!" I yelped. The adorable girl who'd been waiting for me glared directly at my face. As she loomed in closer, her sleek black ponytail bobbed with irritation.

"Sorry, Hana," I said. "I lost track of time in the dungeon."

"Fine! I'll heat up dinner for you. Go wash your hands."

My sister Hana, three years my junior, spun on her heel and returned to the living room. I immediately went to wash my hands, then sat down for dinner. Despite the late hour, she'd set the table with a full spread of food. I immediately dug in.

"Thanks for making this," I enthused. "It's *delicious*. You're the best cook in the world!"

"Where's that coming from? You're being weird..."

Her sharp response made me clutch my chest as if wounded. Across the table, she gave me a gentle smile.

"So, did something good happen?" she asked.

"What makes you think that?"

"You're talking all strange and you came home late, so it made me wonder if something happened today."

"Hmm...well, you're not wrong. Something good *did* happen." Something awesome, actually.

"Does it have to do with dungeons?" she asked.

"Yeah! Something so good that it validates my decision to put the effort into becoming an adventurer."

Her expression eased into relief. "That's great. I'm happy for you."

Hana knew I was a talentless adventurer. She often asked me how things were going in the dungeons, probably out of worry. I was grateful to have a little sister who cared so much about me. I was grateful to have her at all.

After all, Hana was my only family.

A few years back, our parents were caught in an accident during a vacation overseas and went missing. They left enough money for us to survive on, but we weren't exactly living it up. Since I became an adventurer, I had earned us some spending money, but I also needed to buy equipment for adventuring. In E- and D-rank dungeons, those earnings only went so far.

Hana respected my selfish childhood dream of becoming a top-tier adventurer. I couldn't hold anything against her in light of that. Once I made some real money, I wanted to repay the favor tenfold.

"Now, did this *good thing* make you strong enough to take on C-rank dungeons?" Hana asked, pulling me out of my thoughts. She smiled teasingly: she must've known I only just surpassed level 200. C-rank dungeons jumped dramatically in difficulty; an adventurer needed to be level 500 at a minimum to take them on. She had to be pulling my leg.

With the way things were going, it had taken me a whole year to get to my current level. I knew she was kidding, but thanks to Dungeon Teleportation, I could level up much more effectively. I *might* be challenging C-rank dungeons in a month.

"Listen to this. What happened was—"

I quickly cut myself off. Should I really tell her this? The power I'd obtained enabled me to bypass the Span, an obstacle that barred the growth of every adventurer in the world. I doubted anyone would take kindly to me leveling up that way. Heck, people might get jealous or angry enough to attack me. Hana wasn't the kind of person to run around telling everyone my secret, but there were lots of ways information could leak. This secret needed to stay with me.

"What's the matter, oniichan? You spaced out."

"It's nothing. Unfortunately, it'll be a while before I can try out C-rank dungeons."

"Well, I knew that."

"Then don't ask. Jeez..."

Hana snickered. Seeing her smile, I quickly forgave her for teasing.

After that, we chatted about everything and nothing while we ate. Casual moments like this were more important than anything else.

The next day, I made a list of the nearby dungeons I'd beaten before and considered which one I should go to first. In terms of which dungeon was most effective for leveling up, Yunagi Dungeon was my top choice. I could beat it in about two hours. Plus, the level-up reward was five levels. If I beat it five times in

one day, I'd gain twenty-five levels. One problem: out of all the D-rank dungeons, Yunagi Dungeon had the most resources to gather, which meant a lot of money-seeking adventurers would be there. Often, I was one of them. The Return Zone saw a lot of foot traffic too. If I used Dungeon Teleportation, people were bound to see me vanish. Not to mention the possibility of someone noticing my return via the dungeon's teleportation spell multiple times in one day. I couldn't draw attention to myself like that.

I needed a less populated place like Shion Dungeon. I could defeat that one in one hour, but the level-up reward was only one level. Compared to Yunagi Dungeon, it wasn't as effective to train in. Not to mention Shion Dungeon didn't offer as much loot, so the only profit would be gathering a few levels.

"This one, then."

The D-rank dungeon—Yumemi Dungeon.

The recommended level to beat it was 120, but in the grand scheme of D-rank dungeons—where recommended levels could range from 100 to 500—this one was pretty low difficulty. The catch was the vastness of its floors. It would take three hours to beat Yumemi. Considering the level-up reward was five levels, the time wasn't as bad as it sounded, but it was a little worse than other options. In one run, I would harvest enough magic stones to make around 10,000 yen. If I beat it three times in one day, I'd move up fifteen levels and make a 30,000 yen profit.

Usually, the size of the dungeon wouldn't be enough to keep people away from a decent profit, but Yumemi Dungeon was also known for giving few experience points. There wasn't much merit in gathering its resources to sell without other benefits. For my purposes, that downside was actually an upside. Hardly any adventurers challenged it, which meant fewer prying eyes on me and my skill.

"Yeah, this is the one for sure!"

Once I finished getting ready, I hopped on the train and headed for Yumemi Dungeon.

Like I expected, Yumemi Dungeon was a ghost town.

After showing my Adventurer Card to the supervisor, I took the stairs down to the Return Zone. I stood before the Gate then glanced around for any other people.

Nobody was there: perfect.

Adventurers needed to meet at least level 80 to cross the Gate into Yumemi Dungeon, but that didn't apply to me. Not even the Span could stop me from entering. A beat of silence passed—then my skill activated, and I landed on the other side of the Gate without issue.

"Guess I'll get started."

As I walked forward, I recalled the last time I beat this dungeon three months ago. Goblins, kobolds, and gray wolves spawned here. The gray wolves were the strongest of the three.

Short sword in one hand, I moved through the dungeon. I actually obtained this sword—the Yumemi Short Sword—right here. It could only be obtained during the first run through the dungeon: the boss dropped it as a special reward if the adventurer beat it solo. It had the ability to boost Attack parameters by +60, so it was a pretty great weapon to have. I'd loved it since the second I obtained it.

"Here's company."

I raised my short sword toward the direction I sensed a monster's presence. The ash-colored coat flagged the monster—no, *three* of them—as gray wolves. They fought in packs, so they were tough opponents, but...

"Too slow."

I parried a gray wolf and slashed out, inflicting damage right away. Last time, fighting them took a lot out of me, but my level was *waaay* higher now. Those wolves had nothing on me. This was proof that I'd made real progress from leveling up and improving my stats. Talent was important in a battle, but under the world leveling system, boosting raw numbers was the most important factor to growing as an adventurer.

"That was easy," I said, leaving the defeated gray wolves behind.

To keep up the pace, I did my best to avoid pulling aggro from the monsters and reduced my battles to a minimum. Three hours after I entered the dungeon, the giant door to the boss room towered before me. When I touched it, it groaned open with a creak. Good timing; no one else was already fighting the boss. If a party was in there, the door wouldn't have opened until the battle was over. The wait would've been annoying.

"Oops. Should probably focus on the boss right now."

Yumemi Dungeon's boss was a harpy—a half-human, half-bird creature with a woman's face. She had the ability to sing and lull her opponents into sleep, but with my Resistance parameters, her siren song had no effect on me. The hardest part was the way harpies fought in the air, flying around until the last second when they dove in for the attack. Last time, the battle dragged on for ages because of her tricks.

This time should be easier. I came prepared.

I reached into the pouch on my waist and withdrew a palm-sized rock. This Exploding Stone was a magic item imbued with a spell to explode on contact. Exploding Stones came in various strengths, but this one was on the lower end in terms of power. One stone only cost 2,000 yen: not a bad price for a magic item.

"Take this!" I shouted.

I flung the Exploding Stone at the harpy. It struck her with a loud *bang* that shook the area. The harpy screeched as the explosion completely enveloped her. It didn't look like it dealt a huge amount of damage, but it definitely pissed her off. The angry harpy swooped into a nosedive, straight toward me.

Exactly what I wanted.

I waited for the perfect moment and swung hard with my short sword. As a gash opened in her torso, the harpy went down with another screech.

The system dinged in my head.

"Dungeon Takedown Reward: Level increased by 5!"

I clenched my fist in victory. "Yes! Five levels already."

Until yesterday, even if I'd spent all day fighting in the dungeon, I'd only gain one measly level. The speed at which my levels grew now was unreal, but I wasn't going to be satisfied with this rate. No way, no how!

I've got tons of time. I'm going to beat Yumemi Dungeon as many times as I can today, I thought. *Oh, almost forgot.*

In my excitement, I hadn't looted the harpy's body for magic stones. Once I remembered, I made quick work of it with my short sword and found 5,000 yen's worth of magic stones inside. A decent haul.

The soft light of the dungeon's teleportation spell enveloped my body. I mumbled to myself, "It's time, then."

The spell landed me in the Return Zone—but obviously, I wasn't going home just because it did that.

"Time for another round, that is!"

Feeling fired up, I activated Dungeon Teleportation and went back in. After that, I beat Yumemi Dungeon twice more. In total, I grew fifteen levels in one day.

AMANE RIN

LEVEL: 224   SP: 200

HP: 1,720/1,830   MP: 320/410

ATTACK: 460   DEFENSE: 330   SPEED: 480

INTELLIGENCE: 320   RESISTANCE: 330   LUCK: 320

SKILLS: Dungeon Teleportation LV 10, Enhanced Strength LV 3

◆ ⌃ ◆

"On second look, this is wilder than I thought..." I murmured to myself.

At home, I sat in my room and pored over my stats. The morning before, I was only at level 194. In two days, I had climbed to level 224. Fifteen entire levels. This speed was completely unprecedented.

"Now, where should I apply these 200 SP?"

I tapped the skill menu and checked the details. First, it displayed the skills I already had.

> **OBTAINED SKILLS**
> Dungeon Teleportation LV 10 → LV 11 (SP NEEDED: 500)
> Enhanced Strength LV 3 → LV 4 (SP NEEDED: 40)

"Hrm. Looks like I need 500 SP to reach Dungeon Teleportation LV 11, huh?"

That was a lot, but I figured using that much SP could boost my levels faster in the future. Regardless, it was a moot point because I didn't have that kind of SP to play with right now.

I looked at Enhanced Strength instead. Close-combat attacks were the foundation of my fighting style, so raising the parameters for physical aspects was important. The better my physical attributes were, the better I fought.

Still, I didn't choose Enhanced Strength either. I wanted to see the new skills lower on the display. Swordsmanship, Healing Magic, Enemy Detection—there were lots of skills out in the world. I scrolled onward and found what I was looking for.

"Here we go."

NEW SKILLS
Appraisal (SP NEEDED: 200)
Item Box LV 1 (SP NEEDED: 200)

Both skills unlocked for adventurers over level 100, which meant they were intermediate skills. I'd unlocked them a while ago, but I prioritized leveling up Dungeon Teleportation, so I hadn't obtained them yet.

Appraisal would grant me the ability to see a monster's stats and give me information on dungeon loot. It was an advantageous skill to have. General consensus said that at least one person in a party should have it. As a solo dungeon diver, that person had to be me.

Item Box—the other skill on the list—was also crucial for solo adventurers. For any adventurers, really. Item Box allowed the adventurer to store monster materials and other loot in a separate space. Adventurers could use it to swap equipment in unexpected circumstances and collect items they didn't have room for and would otherwise abandon. A common trick of the trade was to store dungeon-dive equipment and normal clothes in the Item Box to change into at a moment's notice.

These days, it wasn't rare to see adventurers walk around town in armor. We sure drew stares though, and honestly, I'd rather stay incognito. So, given the choice between Appraisal and Item Box...

Each one costs 200 SP, so I can't have both. But I'm gonna go back to Yumemi Dungeon tomorrow. I'm in no rush to get Appraisal. Guess that settles that.

I used 200 SP and obtained Item Box LV 1. At LV 1, I couldn't store much, but it would help plenty. I was pleased knowing I wouldn't have to lug my raw materials around anymore.

After that, I ate the delicious dinner Hana made for me and went to bed early in preparation for the next day.

> **DUNGEON TAKEDOWN REWARD:** Level increased by 5!
> **LEVEL:** 224 → 229
> **DUNGEON TAKEDOWN REWARD:** Level increased by 5!
> **LEVEL:** 269 → 274
> **DUNGEON TAKEDOWN REWARD:** Level increased by 5!
> **LEVEL:** 334 → 339
> **DUNGEON TAKEDOWN REWARD...**

From that day on, I leveled up and up and *up*.

Goblins, kobolds, and gray wolves had nothing on me. After I broke level 300, even the harpy boss went down in one hit. As for the SP I gained every time I leveled up, I used that on Appraisal and Enhanced Strength.

I maxed out Enhanced Strength at LV 10 and unlocked better intermediate skills: Herculean Strength, Endurance, and High-speed Movement. I chose High-speed Movement to maximize my dungeon runs. The time it took to defeat the dungeon grew shorter and shorter.

Thanks to that, I defeated the dungeon thirty times in four days. My status morphed into this:

AMANE RIN

LEVEL: 374	SP: 210	
HP: 3,030/3,030	MP: 710/710	
ATTACK: 760	DEFENSE: 560	SPEED: 800
INTELLIGENCE: 540	RESISTANCE: 560	LUCK: 520

SKILLS: Dungeon Teleportation LV 10, Enhanced Strength LV MAX, High-speed Movement LV 3, Appraisal, Item Box LV 1

ENHANCED STRENGTH LV MAX: +100 to Attack, Defense, and Speed
HIGH-SPEED MOVEMENT LV 3: +300 Speed

"This is going well. *Too* well."

My level, stats, skills—they'd all grown shockingly fast. At this rate, looping dungeon runs really *could* take me to level 100,000. Feathery-light hope swelled in my heart.

I had no idea my level-up routine would be interrupted the next day.

When I arrived at Yumemi Dungeon, I instantly noticed more adventurers present than before. *Oh, right, it's Saturday.*

Weekends tended to draw more adventurers to the dungeons. Students and people with day jobs didn't have time to dive during the weekdays.

With the way the level system worked, it was possible to level up by entering dungeons where they could safely explore and fight higher-level monsters without worrying about the danger. Stats gave advantages in daily life, so lots of people did it. Weekend Adventurers, basically.

For those people, the week-long Span wasn't a big obstacle to their once-per-week dungeon diving lifestyle. They could defeat dungeons without any reservations or concerns. Here at Yumemi Dungeon, the monsters along the way didn't give much experience or loot, but the Dungeon Takedown Rewards were decent enough to draw a good amount of attention.

"Better make sure no one sees me use Dungeon Teleportation," I said to myself, heading for the Return Zone.

Careful not to cross paths with other adventurers, I finished four runs. On the fourth, I made my best run time in the last few days. If I kept my pace up, I could break ten runs in one day. With that goal in mind, I headed for the boss floor for the fifth time.

Thump thump thump.

"What's that sound?" I wondered aloud.

Suddenly, several pairs of footsteps echoed from in front of me. I turned toward the sound to see three boys and a girl—around high school or college age—rushing up the path in a panic.

"Run while we can!" one shouted.

"I know! We can't beat that many!"

"*Someone's* gotta survive, at least! Better be us!"

They raced past me. A sense of foreboding filled my entire body as I processed their conversation.

"'Better be us'...?" I repeated to myself. The worst possible scenario came to mind. "No, they *didn't!*"

"*Someone, help me!*" a desperate voice cried, from the same direction that party fled from. Oh, they *definitely* did exactly what I think they did.

I pushed my speed parameters to the limit and raced toward that desperate voice. A few seconds later, I found a cute girl surrounded by three gray wolves. Her equipment suggested she was a sorcerer type—and sorcerers would never survive a dungeon solo. Which meant only one thing.

Looking at her, it was plain as day.

"They abandoned her."

Gray wolves averaged around level 100. That was twenty levels below the harpy boss, but the numbers were the real problem. Three level 100 gray wolves were way harder to beat than a single level 120 monster.

That group used her as a decoy to save themselves. In a dungeon, that was an unforgivable act. I should report them to the dungeon supervisor.

But first things first.

A gray wolf snarled. The girl trembled and screamed as it bared its teeth for an attack. With all my strength, I dashed forward, put myself between the two, and swung my short sword. That one strike severed the gray wolf in half.

"Huh...?" the girl behind me asked, her voice quiet and bewildered.

"You're gonna be okay," I told her, then faced the remainder of the gray wolf pack.

The wolves tried to intimidate and attack me in succession, but none of their strikes made contact. I swung my sword with precision and took the gray wolves down one after the other.

"W-wow..." the girl murmured.

"You're last!" I shouted as I took down the final wolf, two minutes after the fight had started.

Finally, the girl was safe. I flicked the gray wolf blood from my sword, returned it to my item box, and walked back to her. Despite the death of the wolves, she remained kneeling on the ground and didn't try to get up. Was she okay? I thought I'd rescued her in time, but she might've been injured before I arrived.

"Um, are you okay?" I asked. "You're not hurt, are you?"

"N-no, I'm not. My strength just kinda left me... Oh! Thank you for saving me!"

"Sure thing."

I offered a hand and helped her stand, but once she was up, she squeaked and tipped forward.

"Whoa, there," I said, catching her before she could fall.

A moment later, we simultaneously realized that our bodies were pressed together, faces nearly touching. Her cute face was *so* close to mine, and I felt her rapid heartbeat through her chest. Then her face bloomed bright red. She seemed even more shaken than I was. Abruptly, she staggered back and put some distance between us.

Did she hate close proximity with me that much? That kinda stung, to be honest. Still, I needed to apologize for making her uncomfortable.

"Sorry. You collapsed so suddenly. I didn't mean to cross a boundary," I said.

"I-it's fine. You didn't cross any boundaries! Really!" She shook her head adamantly, easing my concern.

"I'm safe, thanks to you. Really, I can't thank you enough!" She must have meant it, since she smiled at me and bowed deeply.

After that, I asked her how things got to that point.

Her name was Kasai Yui. She was seventeen years old, and she would enter her final year of high school next month in April. Since she became an adventurer, just a few months after her seventeenth birthday, she'd been weekend diving.

Hearing Kasai-san talk about this reminded me of one of the dungeon-diving rules. "Oh, yeah. You can become an adventurer at seventeen these days, right?"

"Yep. The requirement just changed this year!"

Twenty years ago, dungeons appeared around the world: as the days and months passed, humanity understood them better.

Rules were established. One of them was that anyone aged sixteen or under couldn't enter a dungeon. Since there was a possibility that someone would die in unforeseen circumstances, this age limit was true worldwide. That being said, sixteen was just a minimum: various countries established their own base ages for their adventurers. Japan was among them. Until recently, there was outcry about preventing minors from entering dungeons. Now, an adventurer hopeful had to be eighteen or older to get their qualifications.

These days though, the strength and numbers of a nation's adventurers was a status symbol. Japan eventually caved to the opinion that they should increase the number of Japanese adventurers. This year, they lowered the minimum age to take the qualification exam to seventeen. The change hadn't posed any issues so far, so there were rumors they would lower the age again to sixteen in April. That recent change was why Kasai-san could become an adventurer before finishing high school, unlike me.

The thought inadvertently made me sigh.

Kasai-san tilted her head at me. "Is something wrong?"

"Just thinking that if the age requirement had been one year lower for me, I could've been adventuring while I was a student too." I steadied my composure. "Why were you here alone, anyway?"

"Well, you see..."

◆⌃◆

Everything she told me lined up with what I expected. "Basically, you formed a party just for today, but when you encountered the gray wolf pack, they left you as bait, so they could get away safely."

"That about sums it up, yeah." Her shoulders drooped.

Jeez, they really did leave her for dead.

What happened inside a dungeon stayed inside that dungeon. No one on the outside would ever know the truth. That was why a crime like this was such a weighty one. To use a party member as a decoy was the crime of all crimes, to be honest. Adventurer laws mandated a minimum of revoked qualifications, and they would probably get slapped with worse.

They knew that when they left her.

I'd report them to the dungeon administrator later. First, I needed to figure out the best way to get Kasai-san to the surface now that she was alone. Though, we were so close to the boss floor. Might as well take on the boss and clear the dungeon.

"We should get moving," I suggested. "Come with me."

"Huh? U-uh, okay!" she replied nervously, following in my footsteps.

A few minutes later, that familiar giant door loomed over us. Touching it didn't open it. Someone must've been fighting the boss inside. Kasai-san seemed surprised that I brought her to the boss room in the first place.

"Are we really going to face the boss?" she asked.

"Yeah. Beating her is the fastest way to reach the Return Zone. Is that a problem?"

"No, I mean, I'm grateful for your help. But can we beat a boss by ourselves? You spent so much energy fighting those other monsters too..."

She must've been concerned about my abilities. I appreciated it, but I hadn't made a dent in my threshold for the day. Gray wolves had nothing on my current level.

The party before us must've finished off the boss because the door groaned open slowly. I turned on my heel and entered with Kasai-san behind me.

As we walked, I assured her, "No need to worry. Who do you think I am?"

"...Should I know who you are?"

Crap. I'd prioritized gathering info from her, so I completely forgot to introduce myself.

"I'm Amane Rin."

"Oh, Amane Rin-san? Ah, I already know an 'Amane.' Can I call you Rin-san?"

"Sure."

"Thank you. You can call me Yui, if you want!"

"Nice to meet you, Yui."

Yui and I entered the boss room. I readied my blade. Watching me strike the dungeon boss down from the air with one blow made Yui gasp and break out in applause.

The second the harpy hit the ground, the system alerted my mind.

"Dungeon Takedown Reward: Level increased by 5!"

The reward boosted me to level 399. Yui should've received a boost too. I saw her smile from ear to ear.

"Thanks to you, Rin-san, I just became level 85!"

"Level 85?"

Hearing that number brought a question to mind. If she was level 85 now, that meant that she was level 80 when she walked in here. That was Yumemi Dungeon's minimum requirement, and nowhere near the level she'd need to guarantee her safety. Lots of adventurers entered Yumemi Dungeon at level 100 or over. Anyone lower level wouldn't even get invited to join a party. How did she manage to get an invite, let alone make it to the bottom floor?

From the look of her clothes, I knew it was possible, but...

"Yui, are you a *healer*?" I asked.

"Yep!" she said cheerfully.

"Ah, I get it now."

Adventurers of many types existed. Knights, tanks, and sorcerers represented a few, but among those, healers were especially rare. Anyone who received a healer skill when they gained their stats had a guaranteed future as an adventurer. Made sense that even a low-level healer would get recruited to join a party.

The soft glow of the dungeon's teleportation spell enveloped our bodies. "Time's almost up," I said.

We quickly harvested the magic stones from the harpy's body. Right after, the spell transported us to the Return Zone.

◆❯❮◆

Once we landed in the Return Zone, I immediately heard the voices of the group who abandoned Yui.

"Ha! I thought we were screwed for a second there."

"Yeah. I feel sorry for that girl, but what else were we gonna do?"

"How will we explain it to the dungeon supervisor? Going in as a party of five but coming out with four is gonna raise a lot of questions..."

They debated heatedly, unaware that other adventurers—namely us—were in earshot.

Yui developed a withdrawn expression. "Rin-san..."

"I know. Get behind me."

I stepped in front of Yui and shielded her from view as much as I could, but they noticed us right away.

"Hey, look. It's Kasai."

"So it *is*. How did she survive that?"

"Shut it, dumbass! Don't say that crap in front of people!"

The boy who turned to yell at his party members turned slowly, deliberately, toward us. A smirk spread across his face. Behind me, Yui gripped my clothes in fear.

"Yo, Kasai. You're good, yeah? We were worried about—"

"Stay away from her."

I put a protective arm out to block him from Yui. Irritation visibly throbbed in his temple.

"Who are *you*?" he demanded.

"Doesn't matter. Yui told me everything. Sorry, but you can't cover up what you did. I'm going to tell the supervisor, and you'll likely lose your qualifications."

"Screw you!"

His face turned red with panic and rage as he reached back for his sword. He raised it and pointed it at me.

"Leader, are you serious?!" one of his allies asked.

"Damn right I am. I'm taking them out! They can't say anything if they're *dead*!"

"You *are* serious."

"Obviously! We *just* got the benefits of being adventurers. I'm not throwing that down the drain! You get your weapons out too! We'll finish this before anyone else comes down here."

The other three exchanged glances, then drew their weapons. They chose their side.

I wanted to avoid costing them their adventurer privileges, but this was something else. How could they think the right choice was to double down with another crime?

"You'll go this far for special privileges?" I asked.

"Hell *yeah*, we will! You're an adventurer. You get it, don't you? Waltzing through a few dungeons gives us power beyond normal humans, on top of money and status. Why would we go back to an everyday average existence after knowing how amazing that feels?"

"I get it. Enough talk."

"Oh? You're more game for this than I thought. Fine. If you bow and apologize, I might just spare your li—"

"I'm saying this conversation is a waste of time," I snapped. "Let's finish this."

A vein bulged on his forehead, like he was about to blow.

"Rin-san..." Yui said hesitantly.

"I'll be okay."

Yui released her grip on my clothes. I stepped toward the four enemies. Appraisal didn't work on humans, so I didn't know what their levels were. But come on, they ran from a pack of gray wolves. What were they going to do to me?

I went to meet them without drawing my short sword. Their leader sneered at me.

"Ha! Another mistake on your part. You think you can beat four of us bare-handed? I figured you were stupid, but this is unreal."

"No. You're the ones who didn't think this through," I said coldly.

The boy snapped. "Talk back again! I dare you!"

I continued, "Maybe you've forgotten with all the blood rushing to your head, but the fact that Yui is here means someone rescued her from those gray wolves."

His eyes opened wide.

"Bet you know who that *someone* is, don't you?" I asked.

"Shut up! Get him, Ami!"

"Fireball!" yelled the sorcerer girl, rushing ahead of them. Fireball was novice-level magic. She hurled a soccer ball-sized orb of flame at me.

"Weak," I said, batting the flame away. It flew in the wrong direction.

"No!"

My HP took a twenty point hit, but it was nothing compared to my full health.

"Now, it's my turn," I murmured. I dashed toward them and closed the distance.

"Ryo!" shouted the leader.

"Got him!"

I planned to take out their leader first, but their tank stepped between us. I wouldn't have minded the switch if not for Yui behind me. If he drew this out, they'd have room to hurt her. I raised my fist to strike the shield as hard as I could.

Watching me rush in sparked his laughter. "Ha ha ha! Idiot! Take this! *Counter Impact!*"

The tank's shield glowed blue. Counter Impact reflected the force of a strike back on the attacker. It was a powerful ability that required MP equal to that of the attack reflected—and that was exactly where its weak point was.

"Haaa!"

I punched the shield with all my strength. The blue light flared as my fist made contact, then it flickered away.

"Wh-what just happened?!" he spluttered.

"Nothing. It's just a difference in strength," I said as I pushed past his useless shield. If the tank didn't have enough MP to match, the skill would fail to activate. His MP couldn't compare to the attack points I used. Nothing more to it.

"You're wide open," I said, and punched him in the stomach.

"*Guh!*"

The hit wiped the shock off his face. He collapsed.

After that, the leader really panicked.

"Oh, *hell* no! Screw this! Why would someone with power like yours even be down here?!"

Admittedly, that reaction was warranted. No one would expect a level 400 adventurer to be inside a dungeon recommended for level 120. Of course, I wouldn't explain my reasons to him.

"Let's finish this up," I said.

"*Dammit!*"

The rest happened in an instant.

The two knights came at me with a combo, but I put an immediate stop to that. Light on my feet, I dodged their attacks, punched one down, then roundhouse kicked the other. Their leader looked dazed and fell to his knees. The sorcerer girl, who hadn't moved since her initial attack, shrieked in surprise.

Three unconscious—only the girl remained. I met her alarmed stare head-on.

"Wanna keep this up?"

Her face drained of color. She let go of her staff. The clatter of the staff on the ground echoed in the empty space as she raised her hands in surrender.

"I'm out!" she declared. "I give up!"

And so, my fight with the adventurers came to an unceremonious close.

I turned them over to the dungeon supervisor. Yui's testimony, plus the sorcerer girl admitting what happened, wrapped everything up neatly. Several minutes later, the boys woke up and confessed. They seemed to have given up on defending themselves.

According to the supervisor, they were in for severe punishment. For several hours after that, the police and reps from the Dungeon Association headquarters interviewed us. Finally, they let us go.

We were free, but I couldn't exactly go back to my dungeon diving. Yui watched me beat it, so I had a witness. I decided to turn in for the day.

Once we made it to Yumemi Dungeon's nearest train station, Yui bowed deeply.

"Rin-san, thank you so much for all your help today. I don't know what would've happened without you."

"You're welcome. Make sure you're well-prepared next time you dive. And choose your party members *carefully*, yeah?"

"I will..."

She probably knew full well what kind of misstep she made. Her shoulders raised toward her ears, as if she was embarrassed. But that only lasted for a second.

"I know! Rin-san, can I have your number?"

"My number?"

"Yeah! I've been meaning to find some adventurers I can depend on, and I'd like to thank you for real sometime!"

"Sounds like a good idea."

I pulled out my phone and we exchanged contact info. Once we finished, Yui squeezed her phone with both hands, as if it were a precious object, and smiled.

"He he he, thank you, Rin-san!"

When was the last time a girl gave me such a carefree smile? I forgave my heart for leaping.

A train approached the platform and interrupted my thoughts. Our homes were in different directions, so this was where Yui and I had to part.

"That's my train. See you next time, Rin-san!"

"Sure. Later."

I started to make my way home.

"Still, the thought of stopping at level 399 bugs me... Yeah, that settles it!"

On the way home, I dropped by Shion Dungeon and did a single run that capped my day at an even level 400.

AMANE RIN

LEVEL: 400   **SP:** 510

HP: 3,240/3,240   **MP:** 760/760

ATTACK: 820   **DEFENSE:** 600   **SPEED:** 860

INTELLIGENCE: 570   **RESISTANCE:** 600   **LUCK:** 550

SKILLS: Dungeon Teleportation LV 10, Enhanced Strength LV MAX,
High-speed Movement LV 3, Appraisal, Item Box LV 1

CHAPTER 2

RAPID LEVEL UP

THE NIGHT AFTER the events at Yumemi Dungeon, I dumped 500 SP into Dungeon Teleportation.

"Dungeon Teleportation skill LV 11."

"Teleportation distance increased."

"Maximum 20 meters → Maximum 50 meters."

DUNGEON TELEPORTATION LV 11

REQUIRED MP: 3 MP × distance (meters)

CONDITIONS: Teleportation can only occur in dungeons that have already been visited.

TELEPORTATION DISTANCE: 2 seconds × distance (meters)

SCOPE: User and user's belongings.

"Sweet! Teleportation distance is 2.5 times farther now."

That 500 SP was worth it, despite it not changing my skill as much as I expected.

Although, when I thought about it, the distance boost didn't feel like a great benefit. All I'd used Dungeon Teleportation for was to bypass the Span. Twenty meters or even fifty meters didn't change that, did it?

Well, leveling up the skill disappointed me this time, but I decided to hold out hope for next time.

Wait a second... That change in mindset gave me an idea!

If what I was thinking worked, I could level up even more effectively.

"Better test my idea tomorrow."

The next day, I traveled to Yumemi Dungeon like always. Once I confirmed that the dungeon supervisor was a different person, I put my hand to my chest in relief.

The day before, I had told the supervisor about beating the boss to make it back to the Return Zone. The same supervisor might've questioned why I was there again—given the Span— but I could fool a different person. It wasn't like the machines that scanned Adventurer Cards logged when we defeated bosses. They only logged when we entered or exited a dungeon.

Bullet completely dodged, I descended to the Return Zone and activated my skill.

"Okay, Dungeon Teleportation. Let's do this!"

The second I landed inside the dungeon, I tested my idea: teleporting from floor to floor. If I could use teleportation as a shortcut instead of wasting several minutes on the stairs, I could finish each dungeon dive way faster.

This wasn't the first time I had this idea: when I became an adventurer, I considered using my skill this way, but I could only teleport five meters. With ten meters between each floor, I didn't want to risk landing mid-air, so I never tried it out. After increasing my skill level to gain a maximum distance of ten meters, there were still a few problems. First, if I landed in a place with a bunch of monsters, I'd have a hard time surviving. Second, I didn't have the kind of MP to spam the skill over and over.

"But neither of those problems affect me now. I have 760 MP! Plus, a hundred Yumemi Dungeon-level monsters could attack me, but I'd still come out on top."

Feeling confident, I put my method to the test.

"Dungeon Teleportation!"

When I activated the skill, it successfully moved me from floor one to floor two.

"Yes! It worked!"

I didn't stop there. I'd only teleported ten meters before, so this time, I tried fifty. In other words, I passed five floors at once. It didn't cost me more MP or activation time than it would if I moved floors one by one, but this way was safer. The less I teleported, the less chance I encountered monsters or other adventurers.

I continued teleporting and finally made my way to the sixteenth—and final—floor. A total of 150 meters teleported, thanks to my skill!

Activation time equaled one meter every two seconds. Altogether, it took me three hundred seconds to make it down here. Including the time I added battling monsters, call it around six hundred seconds total. That meant I finished the dive within ten minutes.

Before this, one dive took me almost an *hour*.

Using Dungeon Teleportation this way cut that time down to one-sixth the usual time. This made leveling up so much easier!

"Hell yeah! I'm gonna grind this hard."

I defeated the dungeon and looped back to restart, hoping I'd finish the next run just as fast. But on my second run, I realized this method had a substantial obstacle.

"I *don't* have nearly enough MP for this!"

My MP pool totaled nearly 800 points. I thought it was enough earlier, but I massively miscalculated my mental math. Dungeon Teleportation required 3 MP per meter traveled. In other words, one dive consumed 450 MP total: more than half of my available pool.

"This means my MP will run out in the middle of my second run. I can still shorten the runs by over an hour, so it isn't a bad thing, but I need enough MP to move from the Return Zone back into the dungeon. There's gotta be a better way to do this..."

Ah, of course! I could use mana recovery potions.

MP was basically an adventurer's lifeline, so any potion that restored mana was naturally expensive. A weak one that only restored 100 MP would cost 10,000 yen. I'd need four of them to beat the dungeon once. At 40,000 yen, that was too expensive: I couldn't invest in that for multiple runs. There wasn't much money in the rewards Yumemi Dungeon had to offer. The magic stones that the harpy dropped averaged about 15,000 yen. One run would put me at a 30,000 yen loss—*waaay* too far in the red.

Buying my way into the higher levels wasn't a bad idea in theory, but Hana and I survived on the money our parents left us and my adventurer earnings. It didn't feel right to dip into it.

"Dang it!" I stomped the dirt in frustration. A shock wave rippled through the hard-packed ground around my foot. "Do I have to scrap this idea...?"

All this improvement to my teleportation, yet it wouldn't take me further. And I was so close to leveling up even faster!

"No... Wait." A solution came to mind. "There's more than one way to solve the MP deficiency. If I can't use mana recovery potions, I can reduce the cost itself."

That I conceived of using Dungeon Teleportation to skip floors proved I was a true adventurer. I thought of it when I was brand new, when I could only move a measly five meters at a time. In dungeons, where stairs extended ten meters, a five-meter warp risked me appearing in mid-air. It was difficult to even test my idea back then: but with all my recent growth, it wasn't so difficult anymore.

This wouldn't work for someone with weaker stats, but since I'd broken level 400, the fall damage from ten meters wasn't a huge deal for me. The answer for the MP problem was right in front of me.

"Better test it now. Dungeon Teleportation!"

Instead of ten meters, I teleported two meters. That reduced my MP cost by one-fifth. Four seconds later, I appeared in mid-air above the staircase.

"Whoa!!!"

The sudden feeling of suspension startled me, but I handled it. I braced for impact and landed gracefully.

"Yes! This should work."

If I preserved this much MP, I could keep each dungeon dive below ten minutes. I should be able to beat the dungeon seven or eight times like that.

If there were any downsides, the main one was a potential awkward encounter with another adventurer. But I pushed the thought away. I'd cross that bridge if I came to it.

After that, I dropped from floor to floor in a flash, and beat the dungeon a second time.

"Dungeon Takedown Reward: Level increased by 5!"

"Solving the problem was great and all, but I don't think I can use this method anymore today..."

I burned a ton of MP between those two runs. I barely had any left. I couldn't get MP out of nowhere, so I switched to the method I used before. At least that strategy kept me at a decent clip.

Twelve runs later, I finished my day at Yumemi Dungeon with a total of fourteen completed dives. My level increased by seventy in one day. With a new level of 470, I had accumulated 700 SP, which I ultimately decided to invest in two new skills.

Mana Boost LV 1 (REQUIRED SP: 200)
Mana Recovery LV 1 (REQUIRED SP: 200)

Like the skill names suggested, they increased my total MP and MP recovery time. Right now, that was what I needed most. If I wanted to keep spamming Dungeon Teleportation, I needed my mana to restore itself without costing me money for recovery items. Besides, even without Dungeon Teleportation, MP was an adventurer's lifeline. The more I had, the more I could do.

"Okay, I guess I'll leave it there for the day. Tomorrow, I'll level up even more efficiently!"

I headed home, all without a clue that tomorrow would be the last day I defeated Yumemi Dungeon.

The next morning, I went to Yumemi Dungeon and utilized the new dive method I'd concocted. In no time at all, I finished my sixteenth run.

"Plenty more where that came from!"

I started early, so by noon I'd accomplished a ton. I had a bit more leeway before I became tired and lost focus. I predicted I'd hit over twenty runs today.

Once I took down the harpy, the usual system alerted my mind.

"Dungeon Takedown Reward: Level increased by 5!"

That marked victory number seventeen. Everything progressed as it always did—until the system said something else.

"You have reached this dungeon's maximum number of allotted victories."

"Bonus Reward: Level increased by 15!"
"You will no longer receive rewards for defeating this dungeon."
"Title: 'Dungeon Traveler' unlocked."

What's this about? I thought to myself. *Allotted victories? Bonus rewards? Dungeon Traveler?* What did it mean? I'd never heard the system say those words before.

Lots of questions came to mind, but before I could figure out any answers, the teleportation spell activated and sent me to the Return Zone. Once there, I paused to consider what had happened.

"Allotted victories and Dungeon Travelers aside, I *do* remember hearing about Bonus Rewards."

Bonus rewards went to adventurers who defeated a boss under abnormal circumstances. My beloved Yumemi Short Sword was a bonus reward for the first time I beat Yumemi Dungeon solo. Other possible circumstances included Extra Bosses, which were stronger versions of the normal boss—things that were unusual, but they still happened occasionally. Bonus Rewards weren't so special they were unheard of.

"Which makes *those* the interesting part."

The words '*Allotted victories*' and the phrase '*You will no longer receive rewards for defeating this dungeon*' drew my attention.

At face value, this meant a single person could only beat a dungeon a finite number of times, and apparently I'd reached that number. I could beat it again, but I'd never get another reward.

I replayed the times I beat Yumemi Dungeon in my head. Before Dungeon Teleportation reached LV 10, I beat it once. After that, I beat it...sixty-nine times. That was seventy times total. The limit must've been capped at seventy runs.

"Considering the one-week Span, it makes sense that no one would beat the same dungeon seventy times. Ten times at most, or they'd move on to the next dungeon once they'd leveled up."

Someone obsessed with a particular dungeon might beat it more than ten times, but the odds of that were super low. Not to mention, dungeons expired around three to five years after they spawned. It could happen for many reasons, but it usually happened abruptly, after a party beat the boss. Because of that, not many people had the time to complete the same dungeon seventy times.

"Is that why no one noticed this rule?" As soon as I said it, I realized I truly could be the first person in the world to know such a rule existed.

"Maybe I shouldn't tell other adventurers about this..."

But how would I explain I obtained that information? Even if the facts got out, it would be hard for other adventurers to act on it. A normal adventurer would have to grind for over a year to do seventy runs. Thinking about it that way, a bonus reward of fifteen levels didn't seem proportionate to the effort.

"Wait, there's a title that comes with it, right? What's that about?"

Curious, I opened my stats display. In the middle, *Dungeon Traveler* was written as an addendum.

AMANE RIN

LEVEL: 570   SP: 1,310

TITLE: Dungeon Traveler (1/10)

HP: 4,560/4,560   MP: 340/1,140

ATTACK: 1,160   DEFENSE: 860   SPEED: 1,220

INTELLIGENCE: 810   RESISTANCE: 860   LUCK: 790

SKILLS: Dungeon Teleportation LV 11, Enhanced Strength LV MAX,
High-speed Movement LV 3, Mana Boost LV 1,
Mana Recovery LV 1, Appraisal, Item Box LV 1

DUNGEON TRAVELER (1/10)

A title granted to someone who has traversed a dungeon in its
entirety.

By traveling through a dungeon a specific number of times, this
person gains special benefits.

I rubbed my chin in thought. "Hmm..."

I got the general idea behind the title. Adventurers obtained them for a variety of reasons. Beating a specific number of beast or bird-type monsters, using the same weapon for an extended period of time, or healing a bunch of adventurers were a few examples. Fulfilling those conditions earned titles that granted benefits like increased attack power or mana efficiency.

But only a small fraction of adventurers acquired titles. Most of them were B-rank or above. I was no exception to that—until now.

I read the explanation below Dungeon Traveler. Apparently, it was a title reserved for someone who beat dungeons a certain number of times. Surpassing that set number was what would give me the benefits. The exact type of benefit was unclear to me. That was as far as the explanation went, which left one possibility.

"This fraction after the title, one out of ten... That must be the number of dungeons I've added to the title. Must mean I need to max out a total of ten dungeons. That's...a lot of effort."

Not that I was upset. Honestly, having a new goal made me happy. Leveling up required me to grind dungeons. Knowing there was something else to work toward kept me motivated.

"If it doesn't matter which dungeon I explore, maybe I should pick Shion Dungeon next. Sucks that beating it only rewards one level, but it would be easy. I'd meet the conditions in no time."

With that, I had my next move decided. Yumemi Dungeon was thoroughly defeated, so I'd go home for the day.

"Wait, that reminds me. Even if I can't get rewards for doing so, can I still beat the dungeon? I might want the loot. I should give it a try."

I traversed Yumemi Dungeon one last time to make sure. I safely made it inside, fought my way to the harpy boss, and, like I expected, didn't receive any rewards for beating the dungeon itself. The teleportation spell activated like always and dropped me in the Return Zone.

"Hrm. I really don't get any rewards at all. Well, Yumemi Dungeon doesn't have much worthwhile loot, so I guess I won't be back. See ya later, Yumemi."

I owed a debt to Yumemi Dungeon. It got me this far. I left with deep gratitude in my heart.

Once I was home, I considered how I might use the SP I'd accumulated, then immediately yawned.

"Way too tired for this. I'm going to bed."

Ten days had passed since Dungeon Teleportation awakened to its real potential. I did everything in my power to speed through defeating dungeons. Now that I'd maxed out Yumemi Dungeon, the spiderwebs of anxiety that clung to me snapped and faded away.

That night, I slept deeper than I had in a long time.

"Wow, I slept *good*!"

I hauled myself out of bed and went to the living room. Hana let out a sound of surprise as she looked my way.

"Oniichan, you're finally awake? You wouldn't wake up no matter how hard I tried. I thought you were dead!"

"Sorry. I was pretty wiped," I said. Then I noticed the table. "Whoa. That's quite the spread you've made for breakfast."

"Um, hello? That's leftovers from dinner. I went through all that effort and you didn't eat a single bite." She began to sniffle.

"You're such a faker, Hana. But I'm sorry, okay? I'll eat."

It made for a heavy stomach, but I ate the combination breakfast and last night's dinner with no issue.

"I can't believe you slept over half a day," Hana said. "Does adventuring take that much out of you?"

"Hm? Yeah, it can. But that's not what happened this time. The dive went so well that I got over-excited and the fatigue snuck up on me, that's all."

"Jeez. I still think you should take a break once in a while. Oh, I know! Do you have plans today?"

"Nothing in particular. I was going to go to a dungeon."

"Did you hear a word I just said? You need a break!"

"Okay, okay, you're right," I grumbled.

Like she said, I'd pushed myself hard lately. Maybe I did need to recuperate. For her to notice I needed it, though? I was glad to be her big brother.

Hana beamed. "I'm proud of you for taking a break! How about you come shopping with me today, so you can carry my bags?"

"I take it back, I'd rather go dungeon diving." Seriously? She had no intention of letting me actually rest.

On the other hand, it *had* been a while since we hung out together. Spending time with her once in a while was nice.

While I mulled it over, Hana gave me puppy-dog eyes.

"*Fine.* I'll go," I relented.

"Thank you! You're the best brother ever!"

My day's plans turned to shopping with Hana instead of dungeon diving. Once we finished breakfast, we took the train to the city center. There wasn't anything in particular I wanted to buy, so I followed Hana where she wanted to go. Then, in the middle of a busy road, Hana made a sound of surprise and pointed ahead.

"Look, oniichan! They're selling crepes. Let's get one!"

"Yeah, yeah."

I let her drag me by the hand into a line at the crepe stand. Hana's eyes sparkled as she looked at the menu posted over the counter.

"I'll pick the strawberry one. What'll you have?" she asked.

"Let's see... I'll go with chocolate banana."

Hana's eyes widened at my answer. "Rare of you to buy stuff like this. You usually pass when I ask you if you want anything. What changed?"

I made a small noise under my breath, unsure how to answer. Before, in similar situations, I only bought stuff for Hana to save money. But I'd been making good money in the dungeons. I could afford a luxury here and there. Unfortunately, I didn't have a great explanation for the change, so I grabbed for an excuse.

"I've been craving something sweet since yesterday," I said.

"For a whole day?! What prompted *that*?"

She looked astonished, but I guess I successfully redirected her.

Once our crepes were prepared, we found a bench to sit and eat.

"Yum! This one's bittersweet," she said.

"Yeah. It's good." Mine was pretty sugary, but delicious. Treats like this didn't hurt now and then.

"Oniichan, gimme a bite of yours."

"Huh? Oh...hey!"

I'd meant to hand the whole paper-wrapped crepe to her, but she opened her mouth wide and bit a chunk out of it instead.

The aggressive move startled me. I stared at my sister with shock. However, she seemed to get the wrong idea.

"What, you want some of mine? Okay. Say ahhh!"

With a sweet smile, she held her crepe out to me. I didn't mean to imply I wanted to try hers, but since she was offering, I went with it and leaned in for my bite.

"Wait, Rin-san? Hana-chan? What are you two doing here...?"

The familiar voice pulled my focus away. The girl I'd met the other day—Yui—stood before us. Hana and I spoke at the same time.

"Yui?"

"Yui-senpai?!"

Looked like Hana was familiar with Yui, too.

"Hana, how do you know Yui?" I asked.

"She's my senpai at school. I'm surprised you know each other. How did you two meet?"

"We met in a dungeon—Yui? What's the matter?"

She was stock-still with a dazed look on her face. My question snapped her out of it and restored her normal expression.

"S-sorry, I shouldn't have interrupted your time together. I just didn't know you two had that kind of relationship."

"What kind of relationship...?" Did she mean the fact that we were siblings? We'd never told her, so obviously, she wouldn't have known.

"I had no idea you were such a *lovey-dovey couple*," she said.

"A couple?!" Apparently, my expectation was *way* off base. Yeah, Yui definitely had the wrong idea.

"Hold up. Hana and I aren't a couple," I said. "Remember how you said you knew another Amane? You meant Hana, right? That should explain everything."

"Oh, now I get it."

Now that she realized we were siblings, I let out a relieved breath.

"You're married students!" she declared.

So much for relief. "Hell no!!!"

I sighed deeply. Beside me, Hana forced a smile.

"Ha ha, always with the crazy assumptions," she said.

"Is she always like this?"

Exasperated, we explained everything over from scratch. It took five minutes for her to understand.

We decided to take things to a nearby diner. Once we were seated, Yui bowed her head apologetically.

"Sorry for saying something so strange!" Yui said.

"No need to bow, and no harm done. We're not mad."

"He's right, Yui-senpai. It was actually kind of funny seeing you flustered. There's no problem at all!"

"Well, *I* have a problem with it!" Yui moaned.

She slumped over the table, clearly embarrassed about what she said. I could have trembled in fear at Hana, who looked sadistically pleased that she'd rubbed Yui's nose in the situation.

The server brought two parfaits to the table while we talked: one for Hana and one for Yui. Hana happily lifted her spoon and took a bite. In contrast, Yui looked apologetic all over again.

"Um, Rin-san? Are you sure I can let you pay for mine? I'm the one who owes you..."

"Of course you can. Sounds like you've been nice to Hana at school, so think of this as a token of gratitude."

"O-okay. In that case, I'll accept it."

While I watched them enjoy their parfaits, I sipped my cup of black coffee. After that crepe, a drink was plenty for me. Hana seemed to somehow have room to spare after her crepe.

"Hana, I'm amazed you can eat so much. Aren't you too full for a parfait?" I asked.

"He he he! Don't you know that girls have a separate stomach for dessert?"

The crepe you just ate qualifies as dessert.

Maybe Hana really had two separate stomachs.

Ignoring her joke, I took another sip of my coffee. I ordered it black to look cool in front of Yui, but damn, it was hella bitter! I snuck some creamer in while they weren't looking.

As they chatted on, Hana and Yui's conversation grew livelier.

"Wait, Rin-san, did you go to the same high school as us?" Yui asked.

"Sure did. Maybe you and I overlapped a year."

"I had no idea. Hey, how about I call you Rin-senpai from now on?" Yui suggested.

Seeing Yui so excited made me nod right away. "Sure. Go ahead."

Names and suffixes didn't seem like big a deal to me, but Yui beamed with happiness.

"I know!" Hana said suddenly. "Yui-senpai, why don't you hang out with us today? If you don't have any plans, that is."

"I don't, but are you sure I can come along?"

Yui furrowed her brow and looked to me. She was worried I would have an issue with it. I wanted to shut down any uncertainty she had.

"Don't worry. Hana can be a handful when she's shopping. The more people to help me wrangle her, the easier it is for me," I said quickly. I wanted to shut down any uncertainty she had. I only put it that way to make Yui feel useful, but Hana pouted.

"Oniichan, you sure do suck."

"Rin-senpai, that's a little harsh..."

Both of them gazed at me coldly.

Uh-oh, did I say something wrong?

We left the diner and went to the mall, where we browsed quite a few stores. As it turned out, Hana wasn't shopping for any item in particular. She only window shopped without buying much. So much for asking me to carry her bags.

Why was I even here?

Not that I was dumb enough to ask the question aloud. If they shot such cold glares at me again, my poor heart wouldn't be able to take it.

"Check these out, oniichan. Which one looks better on me?"

"Pretty necklace. How much...? Oof. I'm gonna pretend I didn't see the price tag."

While Hana held up the latest fashions and asked my opinion, Yui took the accessories and carefully put them back. As I watched Yui, it hit me that I was 'out with the girls,' as they say, so I was something of a third wheel.

Eventually, all that walking through the mall made me thirsty.

"I'm gonna buy a drink," I told Hana.

"We'll be around here. Hurry back!"

I left them behind and spent the next minute searching for the nearest vending machine. Once I found it, I bought a can of cola. As I opened it, it hissed.

"Whoa!" Cola quickly bubbled out. I managed to keep it from spilling on the floor, but the effort made my hands all sticky. Come on, it wasn't like I was waving the can around!

"Better rinse this off."

I hurried to a nearby restroom to wipe it clean and emerged a few minutes later.

"Phew! That was a close one."

I wiped my hands with a handkerchief and made my way back to Hana and Yui. That side-quest took a whole five minutes. I hoped they were still waiting for me.

"Oh! There they are."

Looked like I didn't need to worry. Yui was exactly where I'd left her, though Hana was nowhere in sight.

Wait. Something was off. For a second, I thought Yui was alone, but two guys were talking to her.

"Hey, you free after this?" one of them asked.

"S-sorry, I have plans..." she replied.

"Don't be like that. Hang out with us. We'll show you a better time!"

Clearly, they were hitting on her. Yui was cute—cute enough to compare to pop idols. I doubted this was the first time men had bothered her while she was alone. Where had Hana gone, anyway?

No time to speculate. Yui was alone because I took so long to return. I had to do something about this.

I hurried back to Yui and stepped between her and the two men.

"Sorry. She's with me," I said.

"Rin-senpai...!"

Behind me, Yui sounded relieved, but I remained guarded. Deescalating the situation depended on these guys backing off without a fuss. They made dissatisfied faces.

"She had a guy with her?" one said.

"Whatever. Let's go," replied the other.

They left us without another word, quicker than I'd expected. On second thought, their reaction was normal compared to that group who drew their weapons the minute things didn't go their way. I was just glad nothing happened to Yui.

"Sorry, Yui. I should've come back sooner."

"It's okay! I'm the one who should be sorry. You keep coming to my rescue." Her face turned gloomy, like Hana's did when we were kids.

"Um, Rin-senpai? Your hand..."

"Oh!"

Crap! I patted her head without thinking. That was how I comforted Hana back then. I snapped my hand back, but that didn't change what I did. I hoped this wouldn't upset her.

"Sorry. I didn't mean anything by it. Force of habit."

"No need to apologize! I didn't mind it! In fact, I kinda wanted you to do it again..."

She whispered the last part. I wouldn't have heard it if not for the fact that serious adventurers gained sharper senses than average people. Yui didn't seem to realize I could hear her, so I wasn't going to say a thing about it.

Hana broke the awkward atmosphere between Yui and I, grinning like the devil as she approached. "Now *that's* a surprise! I didn't think you two had *that* going on."

Who knew where she walked up from, but she must've seen what happened between us. My face started to heat with embarrassment, but something else caught my attention.

"Hana, is that *ice cream* you're holding?" I asked incredulously.

She made a smug sound. "How observant of you! It looked tasty, so I bought some."

That seemed to be the theme today. I came to the natural conclusion: Hana had *three* separate stomachs.

After a bit more time at the mall, we decided to head home.

"Thanks for inviting me today, Hana-chan," Yui said. "I had a lot of fun!"

"Great to hear it! Let's hang out again sometime."

The girls said their goodbyes. Then Yui turned to me.

"Rin-senpai, I'm sorry for all the trouble I caused you today. But I'm really, really glad I got to hang out with you. If there's ever another chance, let's do it again!"

"Sure thing. I feel the same way!" I replied, then gave a small wave goodbye.

Hana and I parted ways with Yui and returned home.

At home, I prepared for my upcoming dungeon dive. It really only consisted of spending my collected SP. I was going to Shion Dungeon tomorrow, so it wasn't like I had to do anything groundbreaking.

"Let's see. I have 1,310 SP currently. The SP I need to boost Dungeon Teleportation to LV 12 is..."

My stats display showed 1,000 SP necessary for the boost.

"What? *Seriously*?" That wasn't a typical number to see.

"I don't have a choice, though! The whole reason I'm special is because of this skill."

Despite my hesitation, I used 1,000 SP on Dungeon Teleportation.

"Dungeon Teleportation skill LV 12."

"Activation time has changed."

"2 seconds × distance (meters) → 1 second × distance (meters)."

That was the result.

"This time, the activation time changed?"

Cutting activation time in half would help. Whether it was worth 1,000 SP, well...only time would tell. The display showed 1,500 SP required for level 13. Each level increase would cost an extra 500 per level.

"Considering the next big change to the skill should come in at level 20, I've got a long road ahead, but it's the only way forward!"

I wasn't someone who would waver before an imposing obstacle like this. My conviction was real.

The next day, I went to Shion Dungeon. As an E-Rank dungeon, it was beginner-friendly, of course. Beating it would be easy, and I'd meet the Traveler requirement without delay.

At least, that was what I thought would happen.

"Ugh, this never ends!"

If the title still eluded me after over one hundred runs, there was no way my prediction was correct.

"Yumemi Dungeon was D-rank, and I gained the title at seventy runs. I suspected a lesser dungeon would require more runs than that, but not *over* a hundred."

Leveling up used to bring a smile to my face. At this point, every time the system said *"Dungeon Takedown Reward,"* it haunted me with its voice. When would my dungeon diving end?

Knowing that whining about it wasn't going to help me, I pushed on. All I could do was keep going until the system told me otherwise.

"I've got this!"

I smacked my cheeks with both hands to reinvigorate myself. If a year of scorn hadn't deterred me, I wouldn't lose faith now. This was nothing compared to that!

"Dungeon Teleportation!"

I braced myself and reentered Shion Dungeon.

"Dungeon Takedown Reward: Level increased by 1!"
"Dungeon Takedown Reward: Level increased by 1!"
"Dungeon Takedown Reward: Level increased by 1!"

I kept grinding for four days straight. On the fourth day, I hit 190 runs in Shion Dungeon. I stuck to a steady pace, and when I reached two hundred, the system alerted me.

"You have reached this dungeon's maximum number of allotted victories."
"Bonus Reward: Level increased by 15!"
"You will no longer receive rewards for defeating this dungeon."

"Yeeeeeees!" I exclaimed. My scream was practically a war cry. "Finally, I reached Dungeon Traveler for a second dungeon!"

I took a second and assessed my status. "I leveled up from 570 to 775 over the last four days. Leveling up wasn't my main goal, but after two hundred runs, the jump makes sense. As for the SP I wanted... 2,310 points, huh? Not too bad."

Allocating it would be my next decision. Normally, in the past, I would've dumped it all into Dungeon Teleportation. But...

"No, there's a better way to use these points."

I chose to use them on different skills. Grinding low-level dungeons had its purpose, but it was about time I confronted dungeons more appropriate for my level. No matter how high my level rose or how many abilities I gained, there was no point if I didn't put them to use.

"I'll figure this out once I get home."

I put Shion Dungeon—and four days of totally mind-numbing *trauma*—behind me and made my way home.

OBTAINED SKILLS (CURRENT)

Dungeon Teleportation LV 12 → LV 13 (SP NEEDED: 1,500)

High-speed Movement LV 3 → LV 4 (SP NEEDED: 400)

Mana Boost LV 1 → LV 2 (SP NEEDED: 400)

Mana Recovery LV 1 → LV 2 (SP NEEDED: 400)

Item Box LV 1 → LV 2 (SP NEEDED: 400)

NEW SKILLS AVAILABLE:

Swordsmanship LV 1 (SP NEEDED: 200)

Short Swordsmanship LV 1 (SP NEEDED: 200)

Herculean Strength LV 1 (SP NEEDED: 100)

Endurance LV 1 (SP NEEDED: 100)
Enemy Detection LV 1 (SP NEEDED: 100)
Evasion LV 1 (SP NEEDED: 100)
Status Condition Resistance (SP NEEDED: 100)

Once safely home, I picked out the most viable skill options. They were all excellent skills that would serve me for a long time.

"Before I decide, I should figure out which dungeon I'm going to take on next."

My mind was set on tackling a C-rank dungeon. I'd researched the C-rank dungeons in the area that would be a good fit for me. My main requirement was that I avoid ones with monsters that could inflict status conditions. For solo adventurers, status conditions were the natural enemy. If inflicted with paralysis or something else debilitating, we'd get killed in no time. I would rather face multiple enemies than one that inflicted status conditions.

If my Resistance parameters were high enough, it wouldn't matter, but that strategy wouldn't make me invincible. I could endure the sleep abilities of the harpy from Yumemi Dungeon, but I couldn't imagine what would happen against a C-rank enemy.

"There are skills that can lift status conditions, but right now, it might be risky to invest in a Resistance-based skill."

After all, I'd been investing SP in skills like Dungeon Teleportation, Appraisal, and Item Box—skills that didn't assist in battle. I wanted a skill that would help me fight. Considering my limitations, I found one dungeon that suited my needs.

"Here we go. Kenzaki Dungeon."

The recommended soloing level was 600—fairly low for a C-rank dungeon. A menagerie of monsters spawned there, but they were physical attackers, so it was a good place to polish up my battle skills.

"Now that I have my dungeon, I just need to pick out my skills."

Before, I'd focused my available SP into skills like Dungeon Teleportation, Appraisal, and Item Box—skills that didn't assist in battle. I wanted a skill that would help me fight, something I could deploy inside Kenzaki Dungeon. Evasion was my focus, not attack resistance. I needed foundational skills suited to my agile strike-and-retreat fighting style. For that reason, I didn't want Endurance to boost my Resistance stat. The opposite was true, in fact. It was better to boost my Attack stat with Herculean Strength and increase my Speed with High-speed Movement.

I boosted Herculean Strength all the way to level 4 and High-speed Movement from level 3 to level 4. That cost 1,400 SP altogether, which left me with 910 SP in my point pool. If I wanted to increase my actual strength faster, it was best to choose something like Swordsmanship or Short Swordsmanship, but I paused.

"Frankly, I don't know what kind of weapon I want to main with yet."

I'd used short swords recently, but not always. Previously, I'd swapped back and forth a few times: I used a short sword as a novice, but the low damage pushed me into using longswords. Then, Yumemi Dungeon gave me my awesome short sword as a Bonus Reward. I'd used it ever since.

"Should I spend my remaining SP on Detection and Evasion or increase the level of skills I already have? Maybe I should reconsider once I attempt the dungeon..."

I went over the options several more times in my head. Depending on which skill I chose, it could become a worthless investment.

In the end, I quit wavering on weapons and SP usage and decided to wait. I instead turned my thoughts to Kenzaki Dungeon. I was going to tackle a C-rank dungeon for the first time. My heart thrummed with anticipation.

AMANE RIN

LEVEL: 775   **SP:** 910

TITLE: Dungeon Traveler (2/10)

HP: 6,170/6,170   **MP:** 1,580/1,580

ATTACK: 1,560   **DEFENSE:** 1,180   **SPEED:** 1,640

INTELLIGENCE: 1,110   **RESISTANCE:** 1,180   **LUCK:** 1,080

SKILLS: Dungeon Teleportation LV 12, Enhanced Strength LV MAX, Herculean Strength LV 4, High-speed Movement LV 4, Mana Boost LV 1, Mana Recovery LV 1, Appraisal, Item Box LV 1

ENHANCED STRENGTH LV MAX: +100 to Attack, Defense, and Speed

HERCULEAN STRENGTH LV 4: +500 Attack

HIGH-SPEED MOVEMENT LV 4: +500 Speed

MANA BOOST LV 1: +10% to MP

MANA RECOVERY LV 1: +10% to MP recovery

YUMEMI SHORT SWORD

Reward item that can only be obtained if the adventurer beats
  Yumemi Dungeon for the first time while solo.

+60 Attack

CHAPTER 3

KENZAKI DUNGEON

THE NEXT MORNING, I woke up and summoned the motivation to take on Kenzaki Dungeon. That's when I realized something critical.

"Shoot! I'm in the middle of a Span."

I'd used Dungeon Teleportation to beat various dungeons over the last few days, but that didn't mean the Span itself wasn't in effect. I wanted to face brand new dungeons, but I was blocked from anywhere new until next week.

"Hmm. Should I give up on a new one and tackle a dungeon I've already maxed out? Not that it would change much of anything. Either way, I need to think about how to climb even higher than C-rank."

The more I mulled it over, the more I realized I should hold off on diving for a week. I'd focus on something else instead.

"Only defeating monsters inside the dungeon should be safe, right?" As long as I didn't beat the dungeon, I wouldn't reset the Span.

I set out for Yunagi. It didn't offer a ton of experience, but it still held a wealth of dungeon resources ripe for the gathering. It was perfect for making money.

"Thanks to the diving info available, I scored over 100,000 yen while I was grinding Yumemi. I should aim to beat my record this time." As for how much more money I *could* earn, well, I wouldn't know until I tried.

"Okay, time to go... Dungeon Teleportation!"

The second I stepped into Yunagi, I started on my way down.

I dedicated the whole day to the dungeon before I returned to the surface.

I thumped my chest in relief after I confirmed that I could *exit* through the Gate during a Span. Looked like the Span was meant to keep people out, not in. If that wasn't the case, I would've been stuck defeating the boss to get out, and the Span would've extended a day longer.

Disappointingly, the resources I gathered only sold for about 100,000 yen. Talk about my estimate being *on the money*. I didn't even get a level up out of it! Then again, I knew I wouldn't; my level was so much higher than Yunagi's recommended level. It made sense, but it wasn't rewarding. I sighed.

At least I got a solid workout. Level-wise, the monsters were low rank, but they jangled my nerves when they surrounded me. After so many days taking down a boss in one hit, Yunagi helped me regain my battle instincts.

"Okay, I'm gonna keep it up tomorrow."

During the next week, I continued diving in Yunagi. My movement efficiency improved with the days, and I managed to earn more money than the first. On the seventh day, I finished with a grand total of a million yen and three levels up. In my room, I checked my stats and narrated to myself with glee.

"If I include what I earned in Yumemi, that totals over two million yen. I made a small fortune in no time!"

We could use the money in so many ways, but I knew where to start. Hana always took care of me: as thanks, I wanted to treat her to an expensive meal.

With that settled, I went to bed and rested easy.

The next day, in Kenzaki, I had a date with destiny.

After getting out of bed, I headed for my long-awaited dive into Kenzaki Dungeon. To my surprise, I found a lively crowd.

"They say that out of the people who dungeon dive for a living, C-rank adventurers are the most common. Guess that's true."

By the time they became C-rank, they were well-equipped too. Hardly anyone wielded lightweight equipment like my short sword. No one was going solo like me either. It made sense. You never knew what could happen in the higher-ranked dungeons. Numbers were a fail-safe: no matter how many people joined a party, it didn't affect the level-up rewards from beating the dungeon, so there were no downsides to adding more.

I lined up to have my Adventurer Card scanned. Behind me, adventurers began to murmur.

"Hey, check it out. Isn't that the party everyone's talking about?"

"I think I've heard of them. Everyone who joins has a unique skill. They're total *beasts*, already at level 2,000 after just a year of adventuring. Those guys, right?"

"Yeah. Tons of famous guilds have invited them to join, but they've turned them down for some reason. Why would people like that come to Kenzaki of all places?"

"Beats me. Normally, people like that would tackle more difficult dungeons to match their level."

The conversation prompted me to glance over my shoulder. Those five adventurers stood far away, but they stiffened and turned toward us. Seeing their faces, my eyes went wide with shock.

"No way. They can't be..."

I recognized them. Had they noticed the gossip, or that I was staring? The blond guy at their helm recognized me. His eyes widened in a slightly shocked expression before he started my way.

"Wow, if it isn't Amane-kun! Talk about a coincidence. Never thought I'd see you here!" he said with a flimsy smile.

Bold of him to approach me with that feigned positivity. I wouldn't call him out on it though: I wasn't a child.

"Right. I'm surprised too, Kazami," I replied coldly. I couldn't help it. This encounter brought back bitter memories from last year.

His name was Kazami Shin. He became an adventurer at the same time I did, and once we awakened to our unique skills, we formed a party.

He was the one who created my reputation as a useless adventurer.

One year ago, I'd obtained my adventurer qualifications and began taking on dungeons. I was lucky to be one of the 10 percent of people to gain stats, and I awakened to my skill, Dungeon Teleportation. Until then, teleportation-type skills weren't known to exist. The closest thing to it was the teleportation spell that sent people from the dungeon to the Return Zone. No one could teleport on their own. Needless to say, my skill garnered some attention.

Attention didn't only come from adventurers. I received invitations from guilds and parties. *Lots* of them. One person stood out: Kazami Shin.

Like me, Kazami awakened to a unique skill that pulled invitations from several guilds, but he had no plans to join one.

He told me, "The national guild rankings haven't changed much over the last couple years. That's a shame, so I'm thinking of creating my own. It'll have one requirement, that its members must have unique abilities like us. What do you think? Want to shake up the rankings?"

As a bearer of a unique skill, his reasoning reflected my experiences. I thought like him, believed that I was special, and shared his vision for the future. First, we'd form a party and make a name for ourselves, then create a guild that would gather even more adventurers like us. I didn't exactly have ambitions of knocking the best guilds down the rankings, but I liked imagining us rising up with our own power. So, Kazami and I formed a party.

After that, reality set in.

Dungeon Teleportation proved to have no battle merit, let alone battle support merit. Kazami and the three other party members we'd gathered were different. Their unique skills served a purpose.

Our fearless leader Kazami Shin's unique power was called Lightning Strike. Like the name suggested, he could freely wield lightning, but it was more than that. His capabilities were off the charts. At LV 1, his magic rivaled skills at LV 10. Even more amazing, Lightning Strike didn't consume any MP upon activation. It didn't take much to realize just how *amazing* that was. Compared to adventurers of the same level who were proud to cast their skills multiple times in a row, Kazami could activate his ability infinitely without a care in the world. He said that using it made him a bit tired, but that was no different than any other magic. There were no downsides.

Our other three party members—Satou Yuuya, Tanaka Kousuke, and Takaishi Sakura—didn't have skills like Lightning Strike, but theirs were close enough. I was the only one out of place.

I dragged them down.

After all, there was nothing special about me except the fact that I had a unique skill. The only other skill I had was Enhanced

Strength, which didn't impress anyone. By the time that became obvious, barely a week had passed since we formed the party.

A rumor began to circulate among adventurers. My unique skill was useless and I was mooching off the hard work of the other four.

They made it sound worse than it was, but some of it rang true, so I didn't feel I could argue against it. Kazami told me not to let them bother me, but their words stuck. Once I boosted Dungeon Teleportation to LV 2 and didn't see any improvement, I decided to leave the party. My skill's activation time fell from ten seconds to eight seconds per meter. What good would that do?

With my mind made up, I went to Kazami to notify him of my resignation. I believed it was best for them. But when I arrived, I overheard Kazami and Takaishi talking.

"Listen, Shin. Why don't you simply tell Amane to leave the party? You didn't need to stir up all that talk to get him to quit," Takaishi said.

"Of course I had to, Sakura. We're about to become famous as a powerful party. Image matters! If we cut off a friend after one week, that'd make us seem heartless. It's better if he chooses to leave. Don't you get it?"

"I suppose so. The latter case creates the impression that an average adventurer can't keep up with us. But I'm fine with anything, so long as he leaves. You can choose how to handle it."

"Don't worry, I've got this."

That's how it was.

My party members were the only ones who knew I was useless, but it spread to other adventurers. I should have realized they were the ones behind it.

Why couldn't they have been honest? The party didn't need me. If he'd only said it was a pain to carry me, I would've withdrawn on my own! Despite my anger, I couldn't fully blame Kazami. It wasn't a hill worth dying on, even if it hurt.

The next day, I told Kazami I was leaving the party. I never expected to hear the conversation they'd had. It was surreal to see him act like it never happened. He feigned ignorance and pretended he wanted me there in the party, but once I gave my answer, he dropped the act *real* quick.

After that, I started going solo.

Guild scouts that discovered I switched to solo kept an eye on my skill's potential and invited me to join. I've forgotten their names, but they were famous in their own right. I was sick of making friends, though. I turned the invitations down and spent a while diving E-rank and D-rank dungeons. I focused on proving to everyone that I wasn't useless. It wasn't the first time I'd been underestimated.

I endured ridicule and worked hard to get to where I was today. In short, everything happened because *Kazami* called me useless. I never wanted to see him again, but there we were.

While all those bad memories raced through my mind, Kazami kept talking with that stupid fake smile.

"I never expected to run into you here," he said. "Would you introduce us to your current party members?"

"Sorry, I don't have any. I work solo."

"Solo...? Ha ha ha. Amane-kun, quit joking! You need to be level 600 *at least* to solo this dungeon. Are you telling me you've reached that level?"

"That's exactly what I'm telling you."

"What...?"

Kazami sized me up with doubt. I expected he would. When I left his party, I didn't have the power to grow to where I was now, not within one year, let alone by myself. He had plenty of reason to be suspicious. That being said, my claim wasn't enough to shake him too hard, because his attitude returned in no time.

"Ha! Now, *that's* a surprise. Who knew you'd make it that far? I've been so worried about you since you left. I'm relieved to hear you've grown steadily into a strong adventurer!"

"That's rich, coming from you..." I mumbled.

"Hm? Did you say something?"

"Nothing. I heard you guys broke level 2,000. Why would you come to Kenzaki?"

"Our reason is this girl right here!"

My gaze followed Kazami's thumb over his shoulder, where a girl I didn't recognize stood. Long hair past her shoulders, eyes wide and bright, skin smooth like porcelain: anyone would call her beautiful.

To be honest, she caught my interest. Just a little bit. I already knew the rest of their party members. She was the only unfamiliar one.

"Her name is Kurosaki Rei," Kazami explained. "She's a novice who became an adventurer a few months ago."

"I'm guessing there's a particular reason she's joined you."

"Right on the money! The short version is that she's a unique skill holder. It's a good one. I noticed her talent and invited her to the Kings of Unique. We're here to boost her level."

My eyes widened. If he was here to help someone level up, that would slow down everyone else's level-up rate. What kind of skill did this girl have if Kazami was willing to do that?

"Her skill is *that* good?" I asked.

"Sure is. Good enough for her to reach level 500 in just three months."

"Level 500?!"

In that case, she *definitely* possessed a superior skill, maybe one even better than Kazami's. Could a unique skill really accomplish all of that? As curious as I was, it was bad manners to pry about other people's skills, so I didn't ask.

A moment of silence passed. Kazami must've thought it was time to end the conversation, so he said, "Let's not waste time on small talk. Good luck to you, Amane-kun."

"Same to you."

He and his party left to join the back of the entrance standby line.

With the unpleasantries out of the way, I sighed in resignation—then felt a heavy stare piercing me. I realized the girl from before was right in front of me and nearly leapt out of my skin.

"Whoa!"

Kurosaki Rei. What did she want with me?

"You're Amane Rin?" she asked.

"Yeah. How'd you know?" Kazami hadn't used my given name. Only Amane.

"Kazami-san and the others have talked about you. They said you were one of them, but you were useless."

"Those jerks..."

I couldn't help muttering the insult. I never expected them to smear me *after* I left the group. I didn't know what to think of this girl telling me about it. Back in school, I struggled with reading the room, so I worried I was missing her point.

"But honestly, you don't look useless to me," Kurosaki-san continued.

"What?" That was the last thing I expected her to say. "Ah, what are you basing that on?"

"Just a feeling. But if you want a specific reason, it's because I sense something unshakable from you. It's like you're cloaked in confidence. At the very least, *you* don't believe you're useless."

"R-right."

Receiving a compliment from someone I just met embarrassed me, but not necessarily in a bad way. Though, why was she telling me this?

Wait.

"Is the party hazing you or something? Did you want to ask me for advice?"

"No, it's nothing like that. They're supporting me properly, so I'm not lacking anything. Except, there is one thing."

Her demeanor shifted somehow. I swallowed hard, unsure where she was going with this. If she wasn't getting bullied, great. Nevertheless, there seemed to be something that wouldn't leave her mind.

"Rin, may I ask you something?"

"Sure, what is it?"

I got the impression she was direct with her feelings, so I didn't mind that she used my name without honorifics and addressed me outright. Not stopping her seemed to give her the reassurance needed to speak further.

"What do you think of our party's name...?" she asked.

I paused. In the back of my mind, a year-old memory resurfaced, one where Kazami addressed the party directly.

"We're geniuses who possess unique skills!" he proclaimed. "That makes us the exemplar for all people with skills. In other words, we're practically royalty! So, I think we should give our party an appropriate name. Let's become the Kings of Unique!"

Yeah. That actually happened.

"Honestly? I think it's incredibly cringey."

"Me too!" Kurosaki-san grinned at me and offered her hand.

Huh.

I'd always hated the name, but none of the others agreed with me. In fact, they were all over it. I firmly shook Kurosaki-san's hand in response. Nice to know we were on the same page.

"You're the first person I've shared this opinion with," she said happily. "I'm glad you agree. Call me Rei from now on, okay?"

"Sure thing, Rei."

And so the Kings of Unique Victim's Club was founded. For the second time, I felt the vibe that we were on the same wavelength. What was I sensing?

I left that conversation not entirely sure what transpired. At long last, I entered Kenzaki Dungeon. Somehow, the interior—the whole atmosphere—hummed with a different type of energy than the others.

"Whew...time to get moving."

As I took my first steps forward, I mentally rehashed everything I'd researched about Kenzaki. The dungeon had thirty floors: monster spawns included orcs, horned rabbits, and red boars, among others. They were all manageable monsters, but nothing I could get careless about. The boss on the final floor was a high orc—a dangerously strong monster. The standard battle strategy was to dodge, not defend, which was perfect for my fighting style. If I could defeat the high orc, the rewards would be a twenty-level boost and some Exploding Stones. Kenzaki's Exploding Stones were incredible magic items that rang in around a ridiculous 100,000 yen when sold.

Another great thing about Kenzaki was the Bonus Rewards. Every party member who challenged its boss for the first time earned Exploding Stones. On top of that, if someone landed the final blow on the boss with a bladed weapon, they received a special weapon called the Sword of Kenzaki. The Sword of Kenzaki was a pretty basic name, but it granted +600 attack, so it exceeded expectations. I wanted the sword *and* the powerful Exploding Stones.

After about ten minutes of progress, I encountered bipedal monsters with pig-like faces. My first encounter with orcs—there were three of them total.

"*There* you are."

I raised the Yumemi Short Sword and used Appraisal on the orcs.

ORC

LEVEL: 400

Brown, pig-faced monsters that use clubs and axes as weapons. While slow, one blow from an orc carries exceptional strength.

Level 400? Yeah, I could take on three of them at the same time.

One of the three launched itself at me, a stone club arcing over its head.

"*Graaah!*"

Blocking a stone axe with a short sword would be dangerous, so I dodged, parried, and struck back.

"Hyaaah!!!"

My sword lashed out. I sliced a deep wound in the orc's abdomen, but it didn't die. These monsters wouldn't immediately succumb like the ones in E-rank and D-rank dungeons.

I wanted to pursue it, but the other two attacked me from both sides. I stepped back to put some distance between us, withdrew a small Exploding Stone from my Item Box, and flung it at them. A cheap Exploding Stone didn't do much damage to C-rank monsters, but that didn't matter when my goal was obscuring their vision.

"Graaaw!"

"Groooh!"

The orcs cried out with animalistic noises as the explosion knocked them backward, cutting off their counterattack and creating an opening for me. I slashed with my Yumemi Short Sword and inflicted fatal wounds this time. A few seconds later, I eliminated the third orc.

"Better harvest the magic stones from the corpses."

I also lifted the stone axe that an orc had dropped. It was just light enough to wield with one hand. "Think I'll take this too."

I used appraisal on it.

ORC STONE AXE

A stone axe used by orcs.

RECOMMENDED EQUIP LEVEL: 400

ATTACK +200

"That's a C-rank dungeon for you. Weapon drops from random monsters have three times higher attack than the Yumemi Short Sword."

I'd never used a weapon with such a high recommended level before, but I couldn't choose my weapon based on recommended level. A number was just a reference point: skills like Enhanced Strength could make up for a weapon's lower base attack.

"Hmm, the provided effects are nice, but it would change my entire fighting style. Plus, an attack difference of only 140 isn't worth adjusting to a whole new weapon. Still, I'll pocket it for now."

I used Appraisal on the stone axes from the other two orcs. They offered +190 and +180 attack. Interestingly, it looked like all Orc Stone Axes had different effects. I put the +200 axe away and left the others.

"That should do it. Been a while since I fought monsters so strong."

Over the last few weeks, I'd fought monsters that could hardly dent my HP. Their damage was less than 1 percent of my health, in fact. Here, it wouldn't be strange to encounter monsters that could wipe out 10 percent of my HP at once.

Dang, my nerves really did light up during battle.

"I spent some of our savings on base-level HP and MP potions, but I'd rather not use them up yet." Not until I reached the boss, at least.

The boss—a high orc—was level 600. I imagined I could beat it at my level, but after fighting so many weak monsters, I felt unsure. I decided not to use Dungeon Teleportation to proceed. I'd keep on the path forward, fight the monsters that appeared, and use them to refresh my sixth sense for battle.

"Haven't moved through a dungeon on my own two feet in a long time. Gotta stay motivated!"

With my level head restored, I resumed my trek. Once I adjusted to fighting the orcs, beating them was easy. I ended up fighting five at the same time without taking a single point of damage.

Soon enough, I arrived at the fifth floor, where I finally encountered a different kind of monster—a horned rabbit. Like the name said, it was a rabbit-like monster with a single horn. It stood in my way, alone.

"You're smaller than I expected," I said. I could take a single rabbit down easily. "*Whoa* there!"

In a frightening flash, so fast I barely intercepted its powerful horn with my short sword, the horned rabbit leapt at me. Wow, *that* was dangerous. Horned rabbits were speed-based monsters: one split-second could've been the difference between life and death.

HORNED RABBIT

LEVEL: 400

A rabbit-type monster with a prominent horn on its forehead. It uses powerful jumps to gore its prey. It is tenacious with its strong kicks.

"As long as I know the trick!"

I flipped my blade and struck back fast enough that it couldn't keep up. It squealed as the blade sunk deep and split its body open. This monster had way less defense than orcs. One strike ended its life. I had an advantage since I put such an emphasis on speed. A tank could *take* a hit, but they would struggle to *land* one.

The familiar sound of the system alert dinged inside my head. *"Gained XP: Level increased by 1!"*

"Oh! I leveled up, but I haven't even defeated ten monsters yet."

The experience points gained from the monsters that dwelled in D-rank dungeons or below couldn't hold a candle to the C-rank monsters in Kenzaki Dungeon. I treated them as a blessing and gratefully progressed to the dungeon's depths.

As I traveled deeper, I retained more strength and concentration than I predicted. Maybe my strength had to do with my level increase, but my concentration was probably because of the tedious dungeon grinding I'd done. The experience fortified my mental power.

It was on the fifteenth floor that I encountered another new monster—red boars. They were swift, big-bodied monsters. Scary opponents for sure.

RED BOAR

LEVEL: 450

A boar-like monster with a thick red coat. It uses its sizable weight to its advantage in order to land powerful charging attacks. Its hide is tough enough to use as materials for many types of equipment.

If it attacked by charging in straight lines, dodging would be key.

Right as I sidestepped its oncoming attack, I lashed out with my short sword and landed several of my own strikes. But the red boar's hide was so thick, I wasn't inflicting any damage with my quick moves.

"How about *this*, then?!"

I drew the stone axe from my item box and slammed it down on the red boar's head with as much force as I could muster. Concussed, the red boar tottered sideways. I followed up with a string of attacks that finally brought it toppling down.

"Gained XP: Level increased by 1!"

"Hmm. Red boars sell for a high price. I'd like to take it home, but it weighs too much..."

Furthermore, Item Box had reached max capacity. Digging the magic stones out of its body would take a long time too. My wallet cried at the loss, but I ditched the red boar carcass, nonetheless.

I pushed my way through the rest of the dungeon with determination.

"Gained XP: Level increased by 1!"

"Gained XP: Level increased by 1!"

"Gained XP: Level increased by 1!"

"Gained XP: Level increased by 1!"

Five hours had passed since I started the dive, and I had risen by six levels. At long last, I reached floor thirty—the bottom floor.

"Finally, I made it," I murmured, unsettled for some reason. "I should do a self-check before I lock horns with the dungeon boss."

I was careful to evade the monsters I'd fought so far, which meant my HP was still high. Just in case, I drank a health recovery potion to max it out. My MP was fine since I hadn't used Dungeon Teleportation once. Strength and willpower would be enough. I didn't predict this fight going south at all.

Well...one potential issue was that recovery potions had a cooldown time. I couldn't drink another one until after a specific amount of time passed. The intermediate potion I drank had a ten-minute cooldown. I might need one during the battle. Out of an abundance of caution, I waited until the timer decreased.

"Okay. Time to go."

Once the ten minutes were over, I pushed open the heavy door to the boss room and stepped inside. The sight of my enemy made me smile warily.

"So that's what I'm about to fight."

The beast before me stood at two hundred and fifty centimeters tall, clad in an armor of lean muscle with a club the size of a human clenched in its fists. No monster I'd ever faced looked so intimidating.

HIGH ORC

LEVEL: 600

DUNGEON BOSS: Kenzaki Dungeon

The superior species of orc. A large brown monster with a pig-like
face that wields a club or axe as a weapon. Due to its superb
speed and physical strength, one strike from a high orc will
crack the ground wide open.

The high orc regarded me with an ominous glint in its eyes,
identifying me as an enemy.

"No turning back." I raised my short sword and prepared for
battle with Kenzaki's boss.

"*Grooooooh!*"

The high orc struck first. Shockingly agile for that enormous
body, it closed the distance between us in the blink of an eye.
It raised the club over its head with both hands and slammed it
down with great force. I managed to evade, but the shock wave
shook the ground and pulsated up my legs.

"*Ngh!* That's some strength you've got there!"

If I'd taken that hit, it might've wiped out half of my HP.
This monster's speed rivaled a horned rabbit, and it had *way* more
power than a red boar. Protecting myself by dodging wasn't going
to save me. I had to get creative, and fast!

"My turn!"

I kicked off the ground and burst into my full speed, weaving
from side to side to confuse the high orc. It wielded a heavy club

as its weapon. That couldn't be easy to swing around against a flighty opponent.

"Now!"

With the high orc unable to keep up with me, I thrust my short sword and successfully cut a deep wound in its abdomen. Somehow, it showed no sign of pain.

"Is your body so large that it doesn't faze you?"

The high orc violently and chaotically swung his club. A weapon that big had a wide range, making evasion a challenge. On the other hand, each swing left a wide window for my counterattack.

"Haaa!"

I circled behind the high orc and sliced the back of its right knee. It roared in shock at the wound. If it wasn't damaged by my frontal attack, I would break its joints and stop its movements entirely.

"There's more where that came from!"

After that, "my turn" never stopped. The more wounds I inflicted, the more confused and debilitated the high orc became, which made my attacks even easier to land. Arms, legs, torso, back—I cut into its body over and over.

Eventually, the club slipped out of its hands and hit the ground, maybe because I'd cut its wrist tendons. One strike from me didn't do much damage on its own, but over time, they would add up to a fatal wound. My entire mind focused on reaching the final blow.

The high orc's eyes flashed with something that hadn't been there before—something sinister. I sensed it was preparing to retaliate. It opened its mouth wide and twisted to face me. Its jaws gaped, as if it was about to bellow with every fiber of its being.

"You think I'll let you do that?!"

Before it could get the sound out, I buried my blade in its chest, swapped it to the opposite hand, and used every bit of my strength to slice *upward*. The tip had lodged so deep that the movement tore the high orc open to the base of its neck.

"Gruuuh...!"

Blood sprayed when I yanked the blade out. The high orc collapsed, and the system dinged.

"You have defeated the dungeon boss."
"Gained XP: Level increased by 1!"
"Dungeon Takedown Reward: Level increased by 20!"

"Whew. Sweet, sweet victory."

My fight with the high orc was a landslide victory, with me at full HP and MP. I'd definitely improved, but this victory really made me *feel* it.

"Can't bask in the glory all day now, can I?"

I quickly started gathering my spoils before the teleportation spell could transport me back to the Return Zone. First was the magic stone: high orcs had a magic stone where their heart should be. I carved it out with my short sword. A large stone like this would sell for 100,000 yen, easy. The second item I turned to was the club it wielded. I used Appraisal on it.

CLUB OF THE HIGH ORC
A club used by high orcs.
RECOMMENDED EQUIP LEVEL: 600
ATTACK +400

"Hmm. High attack, but it's heavy and enormous. I doubt I can use it. All that's left is returning to the surface, so I can just carry it. Might as well take it to sell."

The high orc's body didn't have much value, so I left it once I was done. With my spoils collected, I turned my attention to the dungeon takedown rewards.

I'd received my level boost and the Exploding Stone. As a magic item that assisted in battle, it would sell for a hefty sum, but I decided to keep it for myself.

That's when I realized something was off.

"Wait, are those all the rewards? I don't see any sign of the Sword of Kenzaki..."

My research from beforehand said I'd obtain the Sword of Kenzaki if I met the specific conditions, but I couldn't locate it anywhere. A solo first-time challenger who struck the final blow on the high orc with a bladed weapon should've triggered the reward!

Did I have bad info? No, I highly doubted that. I used a source that had never let me down before. Frustrated, I stood there and questioned my memories. Down in the dungeon alone, I had no way to confirm anything.

I wasn't satisfied with the outcome, but I couldn't do a thing about it, could I? I'd investigate once I returned to the surface.

"That's strange. Shouldn't the teleportation spell have activated by now?"

I waited a bit longer, but it showed no sign of activating. As I mulled over what *else* could've gone wrong, the system dinged in my head.

"First-time challenger of this dungeon: Confirmed."
"Solo dungeon takedown: Confirmed."
"Bladed weapon used to defeat the dungeon boss: Confirmed."
"Condition of 'Great Swordsman': Fulfilled."
"Now spawning extra boss: Nameless Knight."

"...What?"

My mind raced to process what I'd just heard. Condition? Extra boss? Why would any of that—

"What?!"

Out of nowhere, the middle of the boss room's floor burst wide open. Something began to crawl out—a creature clad in silver armor, face hidden in a metal helmet, so thoroughly protected that I couldn't see the monster lurking inside. I could sense that the high orc wouldn't hold a candle to this beast, and I was about to fight it.

"This...is a joke, right?"

I grimaced and braced myself for a *true* challenge.

NAMELESS KNIGHT

LEVEL: 1,100

EXTRA BOSS: Kenzaki Dungeon

AMANE RIN

LEVEL: 808   **SP:** 1,210

TITLE: Dungeon Traveler (2/10)

HP: 6,440/6,440   **MP:** 1,640/1,640

ATTACK: 1,630   **DEFENSE:** 1,250   **SPEED:** 1,710

INTELLIGENCE: 1,150   **RESISTANCE:** 1,220   **LUCK:** 1,120

SKILLS: Dungeon Teleportation LV 12, Enhanced Strength LV MAX, Herculean Strength LV 4, High-speed Movement LV 4, Mana Boost LV 1, Mana Recovery LV 1, Appraisal, Item Box LV 1.

THE WORLD'S FASTEST
LEVEL UP

CHAPTER 4

THE NAMELESS KNIGHT

BEFORE MY EYES awaited the Nameless Knight—a secret boss.

Facing him down, I let out a small sound of irritation. Why would an extra boss spawn *now*? Extra bosses were monsters far stronger than normal bosses, and they didn't spawn unless very specific conditions were met. None of my research indicated that an extra boss *existed* in Kenzaki, let alone that I would trigger it!

The truth was, though, I knew the answer.

I must be the first person to encounter this extra boss. The system laid out all the conditions, and they made for an unlikely scenario.

"I'll think that through later."

I had a much bigger problem at hand. Could I beat a creature like this? Appraisal revealed it to be level 1,100. It wouldn't be easy for me to take on at level 808. Regardless, I had to fight it. This was the boss room. The door wouldn't open unless I took it down, or it killed me. And above all...

The Nameless Knight lifted his silver sword and charged at me.

"*Tch!* Looks like I'm doing this!"

Suck it up.

I had no option but to win.

I raised my Yumemi Short Sword and stepped into a fighting stance. First, I intercepted the knight's downward swing with my short sword and blocked.

"Argh, that's heavy."

The weight of the sword itself focused the knight's power straight to the tip of the blade. My stats weren't enough to endure a direct blow, but I managed to deflect it. Unfortunately, the knight's fierce attacks didn't end there.

Unlike the high orc who used the club as a two-handed weapon, the Nameless Knight wielded his sword with one hand. Maybe that was why the time between each strike was so short. His power surpassed the club's power, anyway. I barely managed to parry the attacks, and that left me on the defense. I had to find a rhythm to counterattack.

"Now!"

I slashed my enemy's flank during a tiny opening.

Clang!!!

"For real?"

It didn't work. The blade rebounded off the armor and didn't leave a scratch.

"What!"

With me knocked off my stride, the Nameless Knight followed through with an unexpected attack. It feinted with the sword, then struck with a powerful right kick. Luckily, I managed to block with both arms at the last second, but the kick sent me flying. I heard an unpleasant crunching sound when I landed.

"Ouch…!"

My bones didn't feel broken, but another hit like that and I wouldn't be saying that anymore. My HP had dropped enough to prove it. That one attack reduced me from 6,440 to 5,780 in an instant. That was how vast our strength difference was.

But it was too soon to feel sorry for myself. The exchange helped me understand my enemy. The Nameless Knight's stat parameters leaned toward attack and defense. In terms of speed, I had an edge. That last strike just happened to catch me off guard. That meant I needed to fight this monster like I fought the high orc: evade, find openings, and attack. I'd aim for the knight's knees and elbows. Even with all that armor, those joints should be weaker.

"I won't just roll over for you!"

We launched into a tense second round. I dodged the Nameless Knight's sword and struck out with my short sword over and over. The only attacks that landed were mine. At a glance, I might've seemed superior, but I wasn't. The knight's attacks were explosively powerful. One solid hit could wipe me out, while dozens of my attacks didn't even make him flinch. But I launched my attacks anyway. I pushed my concentration and nerves to the absolute limit. Little by little, my swordsmanship battered against the Nameless Knight's defenses.

"Just a bit more…"

Through my sheer effort, the Nameless Knight's armor grew brittle around the elbows. I *knew* the joints would be weaker. With one more solid hit, I could break the armor.

When my narrow window of chance came, I harnessed my sharpened concentration and focused on my attack. The Nameless Knight's stance staggered more than it had for any of the other hits I'd landed.

"That's it!"

Before I lost the window to act, I swung wide. I put all my strength into striking my enemy's left elbow.

"*Yes!*"

The armor shattered. With that, I successfully cut off the knight's right arm. If I could cut off the left arm too, I could defeat it.

"Wait, what?"

Something snagged my right wrist. It was only me and the Nameless Knight in this room. But he'd moved so fast, I hadn't seen it.

The helmet obscured his expression, but I suspected the knight was smirking.

"You couldn't be—"

Was this part of his plan?!

He knew he couldn't beat my speed, so he sacrificed his right arm to create an opening. He predicted my attacks would amount to one strong hit, so he grabbed my wrist during the second of stillness after I landed it. He chose this strategy knowing his sword wouldn't reach me by the time I dodged away. His silver sword lay discarded on the ground.

I couldn't process that a *monster* had the intelligence and audacity to sacrifice its own body to make that move. Mostly because I was too busy struggling in that same monster's trap.

Monsters aren't supposed to think like humans...!

That was as far as my thoughts went before the Nameless Knight kicked sharply. In my shock, I failed to guard in time. The end of his armored boot caught me hard in the stomach and launched me across the room.

"Gah!"

My back slammed into a wall. Air fled my lungs. Blood streamed down the back of my head. Heck, my HP dropped to 985. That was a loss of one thousand hit points. It was hard to move.

My intermediate-level health recovery potions would only heal a thousand HP. Two would be enough, but I needed time to drink them.

The Nameless Knight lifted his sword from the ground with his remaining hand. He stalked toward me. The moments before he reached me could be my last.

Is this...the end? Do I die here?

I didn't want to face it, but reality was a cruel mistress. My would-be killer drew closer. By some miracle, I could still move a little, but my previous speed was impossible. No chance I would emerge victorious.

"Wait, I have one more option."

There was one last card up my sleeve. An ability only I could utilize: Dungeon Teleportation.

The wall I'd struck was the door to the boss room. Normally, the door wouldn't open unless the boss or the challenger died, but I could probably teleport myself to the other side of the door and escape.

I didn't know what would happen to the boss room afterward, with a surviving boss and no challenger, but I didn't have time to worry.

This is it. I've got to do this.

Running away was my best option, given the circumstances. It was the smart choice. The correct choice.

So, I should, right? Shouldn't I?

A tornado of thoughts spun through my brain. I faced an enemy I had no hopes of beating. The exit was behind me. Using Dungeon Teleportation was the right choice: the *only* choice.

I should—

"Sorry, man. Just buying time."

I withdrew the large Exploding Stone I obtained earlier, infused it with mana, and threw it at the Nameless Knight. The stone exploded with a harsh *boom* and filled the room with smoke, erasing us from each other's vision.

I sensed the knight's bewilderment through the smoke. The smoke didn't just eliminate visibility. It contained a chemical component that monsters hated, which instinctively repulsed the knight.

Then again, the Nameless Knight was intelligent. Within a few seconds, it slashed at the smoke and dissipated it with broad gestures of its sword.

By the time it spotted me, I'd already passed the activation time and said the words I needed to turn the tide.

"Dungeon Teleportation."

When the rumor that my unique skill was useless first circulated, other adventurers told me something:

"You're not suited for the adventurer life."

They told me to quit and take a normal job, that it was pointless for me to hope Dungeon Teleportation would reveal its value through leveling up. Honestly, I'd believed them. I knew it was wrong to have blind faith in myself, my strength, and my ability to make a living as an adventurer.

I put in the effort anyway.

It didn't matter what was right. It didn't matter how foolish I was. It was more important to me that I believed in myself and walked the path that was true to me. I *felt* it.

In this moment of life or death, with everything on the line, the same feeling surged inside me. Using Dungeon Teleportation to turn tail and run was *not* the right decision!

If I was going to bow to someone else's idea of what was right, kneel in despair, or stop when the dream became difficult...

"Then I would've stopped a long time ago!"

Hearing my words, the Nameless Knight—whom I now stood behind—jerked to look over his shoulder in surprise. He reacted too late. I raised the Yumemi Short Sword with both hands.

I did two things in the time between throwing the Exploding Stone and activating Dungeon Teleportation. First, I drank my health recovery potion and restored my HP to 1,985. Second, I opened my stats menu and chose a skill to level up. I used 1,100 SP to boost Herculean Strength from LV 4 to LV 6, which raised my attack boost from +500 to +1,050. Simple numbers.

As if I would use Dungeon Teleportation to *leave the room*! Instead, I teleported behind the Nameless Knight. I had created an opening for a critical strike.

Dungeon Teleportation's activation time was too long to make it viable in battle multiple times in a row. This was my last chance, and the time to strike back.

"Take this!!!"

I thrust every fiber of my being into the strike and sunk the blade of my Yumemi Short Sword into the knight's defenseless back. Unlike the scratches that took all of my effort, this time, a large crack split the armor. Maxing out my attack power paid off.

Actually, was my output *too* high? My blade cracked from the stress of the attack. Pieces of it broke off and crumbled to the ground. Despite that, I didn't relent.

"We're not done yet!"

I withdrew the stone axe from my Item Box and swung that next. It didn't handle like the short sword, but darn if it didn't do a better job breaking the knight's armor! My prediction was right on target. The stone axe made the back of the Nameless Knight's armor fall off in chunks.

"Think we can end this in one blow?!"

The Nameless Knight didn't take my assault lying down. Shockingly, he turned to face me directly, even as his armor crumbled. But I had learned from my last mistake.

"I'm taking your other arm too!"

Before he could attack, I brought the stone axe down on his left arm. The armor snapped off and the left arm, along with the sword, flew into the air. With both arms gone, he couldn't wield a weapon against me.

Any other enemy would've given up in that state, but the Nameless Knight let out a great bellow, and the eyes inside his armor flared red. Drawing near death must have snapped his restraints. However, I wasn't about to give him another shot at me!

"Now it's over."

I tossed the stone axe aside, snatched the knight's sword from mid-air with both hands, and raised it overhead. There was no time to use Appraisal, but I could tell how powerful it was from its previous wielder. The Yumemi Short Sword and the stone axe couldn't compare to the shocking power that flowed from the sword and into me.

My strength was about to reach a whole new level.

The Nameless Knight abandoned all reason, operated solely on instinct, and launched itself at me with a roar.

I roared back.

The rest was over in a flash. I swung the sword straight down in a simple, direct attack. That simplicity allowed me to pour every ounce of my new potential into one blow.

The Nameless Knight split into two pieces. He fell, and the only one left standing was me, with his sword in my hands.

As I stabbed the ground with the sword and used it like a cane to support my weary body, I gave the snuffed out enemy my parting words.

"You are by far the greatest enemy I've ever encountered, Nameless Knight."

A string of alerts came through the system.

"You have defeated the extra boss."
"Gained XP: Level increased by 52!"
"Extra boss takedown reward: Level increased by 30!"
"Title: 'Nameless Swordsman' unlocked."

The maximum experience for defeating a higher-rank enemy, equaling fifty-two levels, and another thirty levels for defeating the extra boss: a grand total of eighty-two levels. Normal adventurers would consider this result beyond their expectations, but I wasn't exactly thrilled. I could've accomplished such numbers in a D-rank dungeon *without* risking my life. The only upside was the loot.

I used Appraisal on my new sword.

> **SWORD OF THE NAMELESS KNIGHT**
> A sword used by the Nameless Knight.
> **RECOMMENDED EQUIP LEVEL:** 1,100
> **ATTACK** +1,100
> When an enemy (human or monster) is of a higher level than the wielder, all parameters except HP and MP increase by 20% each.

So, this was the powerful Sword of the Nameless Knight. The name was a little long, so I shortened it to Nameless.

Nameless was a fairly high-performance sword. It passively boosted attack by 1,100, and if my enemy happened to be stronger than me, it would give me a 20 percent boost to all stats except my HP and MP. Undoubtedly, I would face stronger enemies in the future. This sword promised to come in handy.

The recommended level of 1,100 was above mine but handling it didn't seem too demanding. My investment in skills boosting my attack parameters must be behind that. Either way, this weapon was worth having as I moved forward, whether I used it now or after I hit level 1,100. I trusted it'd become a faithful partner.

"Though, this cost me my Yumemi Short Sword..."

Until today, *that* weapon had been my trusty partner. Now, it was broken, and I felt a small pang of loneliness.

"Thanks for everything," I told it. I knew my final words were pointless, but a sense of peace settled over me once I said them.

I turned my attention to the title I'd gained, Nameless Swordsman, and the details that came with it.

NAMELESS SWORDSMAN
A title given to someone who relied solely on their blade and their own strength to overcome a difficult enemy.
When the owner of this title levels up, the equipped bladed weapon also gains extra features.
If the owner of this title possesses skills related to bladed weapons, the effects of this title will not manifest.

This was a surprise.

"Leveling up improves the weapon too? Is it just me or is this *awesome?*"

For example, if I leveled up while wielding Nameless, did that mean it would boost the base attack or gain special abilities? If it did, this title could be a game changer.

"The condition is harsh, though."

If I acquired skills related to bladed weapons, the effects of the title wouldn't manifest. If I wanted this title to benefit me, I could never invest in sword-related skills while wielding it.

As much as never obtaining those skills would pain me, they weren't entirely necessary. My fighting style was divergent from normal knights anyway. If I truly needed those skills in the future, I'd just abandon the title's effects.

"At any rate, I'll gladly put this sword to use," I said a bit breathlessly.

Sad to say, I didn't retrieve a magic stone from the Nameless Knight's body. Bisecting the knight seemed to have destroyed the stone. It was a waste, but there was no point in dwelling on things I couldn't change.

"Almost time to go."

The return spell began to activate, so I hurried to organize everything. I deposited the magic stones I collected earlier, the Orc Stone Axe, the Club of the High Orc, and Nameless into my Item Box, filling it to capacity just in time. The teleportation spell kicked in and delivered me to the Return Zone.

After that, I sold the dungeon materials I'd gathered except for Nameless. Even if I still carried it, I wouldn't have sold the valuable Exploding Stone. It came in handy to have one. I could find spares to sell another time, and there'd be plenty of dungeons to defeat moving forward.

In the end, I gained 112 levels and 720,000 yen. Finally, my harrowing day in Kenzaki Dungeon was over.

AMANE RIN

LEVEL: 890   SP: 1,010

TITLES: Dungeon Traveler (2/10), Nameless Swordsman

HP: 2,640/7,100   MP: 1,770/1,800

ATTACK: 1,790   DEFENSE: 1,450   SPEED: 1,870

INTELLIGENCE: 1,250   RESISTANCE: 1,320   LUCK: 1,220

SKILLS: Dungeon Teleportation LV 12, Enhanced Strength LV MAX,
        Herculean Strength LV 6, High-speed Movement LV 4,
        Mana Boost LV 1, Mana Recovery LV 1, Appraisal, Item Box LV 1

CHAPTER 5

SOMEONE WITH THE SAME DREAM

WITH THE VICTORY over the Nameless Knight under my belt and worn out from a day full of unexpected turns, I went straight home.

The day after, I returned to Kenzaki with a full stomach and ready for action. Obviously, my goal was to boost my level, but before that, I wanted to check if Nameless would be a viable weapon for my fighting style.

Considering Nameless's abilities, it was a shame to question things, but I was being realistic. Its recommended level was 1,100, and the fact was I just wasn't there yet. One successful strike against the Nameless Knight did not a good fit for my main weapon make. To test it out, I equipped it and entered the dungeon.

Two and a half hours elapsed as I worked through Kenzaki, fighting my way past the dungeon's full menagerie of beasts. Eventually, I reached the fifteenth floor.

"Think I've learned how suitable this weapon is by now."

I sat down in an area without monsters and checked my stat screen. My HP had fallen from 7,100 to 6,680 points.

"Hmm. No matter how hard I try, I take damage if I equip Nameless. On the other hand, it heavily boosts my attack. Pros and cons, I guess."

I'd managed so far by two-handing Nameless. My boosted attack helped me cut monsters in half and eliminate them in one hit. The problem was that it also dulled my swift movement.

"Didn't bother me when I killed the Nameless Knight with this, but that might be because he was a higher level than me and the extra stat boosts kicked in."

The monsters today were lower than my level. Without the stat boosts, I felt the weight of that recommended level, not to mention the difficulty of shifting from a short sword to a longsword. My speedy fighting style didn't suit a cumbersome blade. After considering a few angles, I could see potential in wielding Nameless, but using it was too tricky for the moment.

"Oh well. Gotta go back to the surface and buy myself a short sword."

Fortunately, I didn't have swordsmanship or short sword-related skills, so I wasn't restricted by weapon type. I could swap between short and longswords whenever the situation called for it.

I traveled through the dungeon to the surface with my new direction in mind. My equipment was enough to defeat the high orc, but if I accidentally triggered the extra boss, I wouldn't get off so easily. Next time I saw him, I wanted to be at my best.

In less than two hours, I made my way out of the dungeon and headed for a store selling adventurer weapons. Kenzaki Dungeon lay close to the city center, which meant I reached the store within ten minutes.

Once I entered, a saleswoman smiled at me and said, "Welcome, sir. May I see your Adventurer Card?"

"Sure."

Purchasing adventurer weapons required adventurer qualifications, so salespeople would check our Adventurer Cards upon entry.

Once she checked mine, she nodded.

"A D-rank adventurer then. Our store carries many products suited for anyone from E-rank to C-rank, so I think something's bound to catch your eye. The D-rank products are right over here."

As the saleswoman spoke, I realized something.

Uh-oh. My card only has my D-rank progress recorded.

To update the list of defeated dungeons on my Adventurer Card, I'd need to talk to a dungeon supervisor and have them verify my takedown rewards after I beat the dungeon. I cleared the prerequisites yesterday, but *certain circumstances* kept me from seeking verification.

If I told a supervisor that I'd defeated a dungeon, they would know I was subject to the Span and unable to enter a dungeon for a week. It would completely blow my cover if I entered a dungeon anyway. That was why my dungeon list only showed up to the D-rank Yunagi Dungeon. She had no way of knowing I was ready for a C-rank weapon.

"No, thank you. I need something from this section here," I replied.

"Pardon me, sir, but that's the C-rank section..."

She sounded perplexed, but I ignored her confusion and crossed to that section. Numerous weapons were spread neatly inside specialized glass cases.

"Hmm, which one should I pick?"

A versatile short sword was my goal, but C-rank weapons were rather pricey. The cheapest one topped a million yen. This would be no small purchase. I continued to browse, this time using Appraisal.

"Makes sense the ones with abilities beyond attack boosts would be expensive. They're appealing for sure, but I don't think I need extras right now—oh!"

I asked the saleswoman to withdraw a weapon that caught my interest. The shape and grip reminded me of my trusty Yumemi Short Sword. I liked it a lot.

KIRIKUJI SHORT SWORD

Reward item that can only be obtained if the adventurer defeats the Kirikuji Dungeon boss while solo.

RECOMMENDED EQUIP LEVEL: 800

ATTACK +500

"No special abilities, but the features are nice, and the level limits work for me. As for the price...two million yen? Ouch."

But I *could* afford it. If I beat Kenzaki a few times, I'd earn the money back.

Yeah, the Kirikuji Short Sword felt right for me.

"S-sir, I think you should reconsider," the saleswoman said restlessly when she realized my preference. "That short sword is an excellent choice, but it is quite costly and challenging for a D-rank adventurer to handle."

She wasn't wrong: for most D-rank adventurers, two million yen would wipe out their savings, and I'd waste that money on an incompatible weapon. She could've prioritized the store's profits and remained silent, but she didn't. Any salesperson who went out of their way to caution a customer was an honest person.

"It's all right," I assured her. "I understand how much this sword costs. Speaking of money—"

"Oh?"

I withdrew a stack of cash from my Item Box: two million yen in total. Her eyes widened.

"I can pay all at once," I said.

She gawked for a second, then she regained her professional saleswoman smile and happily said, "Thank you for your purchase!"

With the Kirikuji Short Sword in hand, I once again faced Kenzaki. The return trip was smooth through the fifteenth floor, where I encountered a red boar.

"Ha!"

As I slid forward, my blade cut deep into the boar's hide and opened a gash in its side. My level, skills, *and* weapon had changed.

Unlike the last time I fought one of these, I easily defeated it with a short sword. Once again, I considered the high resale value of red boars versus the challenge of storing something so large. After the pile of money I spent on the short sword, I wanted to harvest as much material as I could. I'd always need more equipment and magic items in the future.

"Wondered when I should level up my Item Box skill. Seems that time is now!"

I used 1,000 SP to boost Item Box from LV 1 to LV 3, significantly increasing its storage capacity. Then, before the dungeon could absorb the red boar's corpse, I deposited it into my expanded Item Box. I had room to spare. Farming red boars was now an option.

"Off I go again!"

Excited, I set off for the deepest level. I reached the thirtieth floor in three hours thanks to my now-familiar new short sword. I leveled up twice on the way as well.

The boss room door stood as tall as ever. The urge to push it open with both hands rose within me.

"I should change my weapon first."

I opened the Item Box and swapped out the Kirikuji Short Sword for Nameless. The main reason for the swap was my new title from defeating the Nameless Knight.

NAMELESS SWORDSMAN
A title given to someone who relied only on their blade and their own strength to overcome a difficult enemy.

> When the owner of this title levels up, the equipped bladed
> weapon also gains extra features.
> If the owner of this title possesses skills related to bladed
> weapons, the effects of this title will not manifest.

Whenever I leveled up, this title would level up my equipped weapon too.

"Nameless is the superior weapon between the two. I'll use this one just for defeating bosses and increase its utility over time."

Since I wasn't the recommended level, I wouldn't have perfect mastery over Nameless, but this was an investment in my future.

"Okay, time to go."

I strode into the boss room, where the high orc—a monster with the strength to pound the earth into dust—stood before me.

Not that I planned to lose.

"Gimme all you've got."

The battle began when the high orc violently swung its club. Last time, I evaded and counterattacked every strike, but this time, Nameless's size slowed me down. Still, I wasn't at a disadvantage. Even with hampered speed, my attack stat was *way* higher. I could fight it head-on!

"Try *this* on for size!"

I swung Nameless in an upward arc and knocked the club out of its hands. The high orc staggered backwards with a shocked growl, as if it didn't expect to be outmatched in strength. Yeah, I had the speed cut, but with attack this high, who needed speed? One hit at full power was plenty to maim the orc.

"Take this!" I chopped across the high orc's massive body.

"*Groooooh!*" The high orc roared in pain. The damage was colossal. This method was going to be *very* effective.

"How many more hits can you take, huh?"

For three minutes, I maneuvered to hack at it again and again. Hit number eight was the fatal blow.

"*You have defeated the dungeon boss.*"

"*Gained XP: Level increased by 2!*"

"*Dungeon Takedown Reward: Level increased by 20!*"

"Doesn't look like I'll be fighting the extra boss this time. Figures," I said to myself while collecting the Exploding Stone takedown reward. It made sense that I wouldn't witness abnormal events like that daily.

"All right, if my level went up by twenty-two, how much did my title affect my weapon?" I used Appraisal to check.

SWORD OF THE NAMELESS KNIGHT
A sword used by the Nameless Knight.
RECOMMENDED EQUIP LEVEL: 1,120
ATTACK +1,120
When an enemy (human or monster) is of a higher level than the
     wielder, all parameters except HP and MP increase by 20% each.

"The attack boost raised by twenty points. That's a decent amount."

Based on that, I assumed adding one level meant adding

one attack for any future levels I gained. It truly *was* an outstanding title.

"Oops. Better collect my prize."

I put a lid on the analytics and removed the magic stone from the high orc's body. As usual, the teleportation spell activated and dropped me back in the Return Zone.

"What time is it, anyway?"

I checked my watch. It was only a little past four in the afternoon. I hadn't yet broken a sweat, so I should go for one more run. In fact, could I possibly speed run it four or five times if I used Dungeon Teleportation?

I glanced around the Return Zone, and once I was sure there weren't any adventurers nearby, I entered Kenzaki again.

"Dungeon Teleportation!"

Once safely inside, I looked for a good spot to use it again.

"Rin?"

The sound of my own name startled me. I turned to find the girl I'd met yesterday, Kurosaki Rei, standing there. She grasped an unusual sword with a yellow blade that seemed as if it was quivering. Just my imagination? That question would have to wait for later.

"I wondered who would recognize me. Bit soon for a reunion, don't you think?" I replied.

She nodded, expression unreadable. "Yeah. We only met yesterday."

She'd brimmed with high spirits when we founded the Kings of Unique Victim's Club the day before, but today she was as blank as white marble. Something about the change bothered me.

"You're not with Kazami and the others today," I said.

"No. I can't expect them to carry me. We went down to the twentieth floor yesterday, but I realized I could go as far as the tenth floor and level up by myself."

"Makes sense," I said with a nod.

If I recalled correctly, Kazami said her level was over 500. Even if it was difficult for her to defeat a level 600 high orc, the weaker monsters on the early floors might be easy for her.

That being said, they didn't always attack adventurers one by one; I couldn't say for certain whether she'd be safe. Despite that, when sizing her up, I sensed she had her bearings beneath her.

I had to be more careful knowing Rei was inside the dungeon. I wanted to grind Kenzaki, but if we met again as I cycled through, she might suspect me of something.

"Well, I'd better get going—huh?"

As I'd tried to say goodbye, she grabbed my hand. What did she want?

She stared at me with her strong-willed eyes while I stood perplexed.

"This is an opportunity," she whispered. Her lips were moist, and the color of cherry blossoms. "Rin, come with me."

I scrambled for a reply, but the only thing that came out of my mouth was one dopey word.

"What?"

◆⌃◆

Rei offered to run the dungeon together, and I ended up agreeing. Couldn't say her pretty eyes had nothing to do with it, but more than that, I was interested in seeing her power in action.

Several minutes later, she and I reached the fifth floor. It'd been three months since she became an adventurer. How was she already level 500? I could learn the answer by fighting monsters with her. Plus, I was curious why *she* wanted to traverse this dungeon with *me*.

We walked together in awkward silence. Neither of us were the type to initiate conversation, it seemed. I didn't mind if we stayed silent, but if we didn't understand one another, we might end up in complete disarray during a monster encounter. Coordinating our battle plan could be a matter of survival.

Rei was the one who invited me, so it made sense that she'd be the one to start bridging the gap, but she wasn't budging. Maybe that was my job as the older one.

Wait, *was* she younger than me? Thinking back, she'd only become an adventurer recently, but I didn't actually ask her age. That gave me somewhere to start.

"So, Rei. How old are you? Got any hobbies?"

The second I said it, I realized my question sounded like an icebreaker you'd say on a blind date.

I glanced at Rei. She stared at the ground, tight-lipped. Did I pick the wrong topic? I hoped she simply had something on her mind. A few seconds later, she faced me with a battle-ready look on her face and spoke with the force of an accusatory finger.

"I'm seventeen. My hobbies are...*a secret.*"

Apparently, our current relationship wasn't close enough to warrant telling me more than her age.

"What about you?" she asked.

My turn in the hot seat then. "I'm nineteen. My hobbies are..."

It was hard being on the receiving end of that question. These days, dungeon diving consumed my life. Any spare time I had I spent with Hana, and I couldn't admit that! It was *not* cool, and it might imply an unhealthy obsession with my sister.

I reached back to my junior high school days for an answer.

"I'm into manga and video games and stuff. Too busy for them recently though."

"O-oh."

For some reason, my answer made her tense. Did she think poorly about my choice of hobbies? Sure, they were in the past for me, but they were nothing anyone should be prejudiced about. Well, whatever. Everyone was entitled to their opinion. If I changed the topic, I could cut through the weirdness.

"S-so, which ones are your favor—" she began.

"Monsters will spawn at any moment. Let's stay alert," I said.

Whoops, spoke over her.

"Sorry, I didn't mean to interrupt. What were you trying to say?"

"Nothing," she mumbled. "Let's pick up the pace."

I turned to her in confusion, but she hurried ahead of me. She said it was nothing, so I took her at her word and followed after her. A few minutes later, as I predicted, we encountered a monster. Four, in fact. A group of orcs bearing stone axes.

I raised my Kirikuji Short Sword. Rei lifted her special, yellow-bladed sword.

"I'll take the two on the left," I said.

"Got it. I'll take the ones on the right."

We didn't know each other's abilities or fighting style yet, so tackling a few on our own was the safest option. Rei nodded at me and appeared to share the opinion.

The battle began. I mustered a burst of speed, charged the group of orcs, and sliced through them before they could react.

"Huh?"

I felt the impact of slicing through the orcs, but something was abnormal about the sensation. Was it just me, or were their hides harder than usual?

"Groooh!"

"Rargh!"

The pace of the battle didn't allow more time to think. The two orcs ran at me in formation. I sidestepped the first one's stone axe, then blocked the second one's axe with my short sword. Again, something felt off.

"Why is it so heavy?!"

The shock of the unexpectedly strong strike forced me to deflect it off the flat of my sword, but the impact knocked me down. I hit the ground with a thud.

"What in the world?"

By then, I knew for sure these orcs were irregular. I used Appraisal to figure out why.

ORC

LEVEL: 600

A large brown monster with a pig-like face that wields a club or axe as a weapon. While slow, one strike from an orc carries immense force.

"Level 600?!"

That number made no sense for a floor this close to the surface, but there they were, right in front of me. What could've caused this? I had no idea, but with a level like that, I couldn't underestimate my opponents. I had to attack the same way I attacked the high orc—no, the same way I attacked the Nameless Knight!

"Here goes nothing."

This was my first fight at full power since the massive level up yesterday. When I reached deep inside myself, I summoned more speed than I imagined.

I let out a battle cry. Before the orcs could react, I struck the first one in the chest, throwing my whole body's weight behind my sword. The orc crumpled to the ground. Was that it?

A snarl rang out behind me.

"Nice try!"

The second orc saw the exchange and tried to surprise me, but I deflected the beast's crude stone axe and glided into a powerful swing. The edge of the blade ripped the orc's throat open.

I'd defeated my opponents, but we weren't out of the woods yet.

"Rei, I'm coming to assist!"

Against two orcs far over her level, Rei could be in a tight spot by herself. At least, that was what I thought until I spotted her.

"O sacred wind, sever my enemies!" she said.

"Huh?"

I gaped at her. Five meters stood between Rei and her two orcs, but she swung her sword anyway. What was her strategy?

Suddenly, the blade of her sword elongated, extending the reach of her attack. It lopped the heads off the orcs with obscene ease. In the next second, the blade retracted those extra meters and returned to its normal length. Rei's expression remained neutral, as if she was watching the clouds pass by high above—and not the climax of a battle.

Wait, wait, wait. What *was* that?

"Is that sword your..." I trailed off.

She seemed to understand what I wanted to ask.

"Yes, it's my unique skill, 'Magic Sword,'" she said with a nod. "I can create swords with special abilities. I made this sword using the wind as inspiration. It extends quite far, so it's rather convenient."

It was a modest synopsis of her abilities, but she'd underlined how incredible her skill really was. "Convenient" didn't begin to cover the scope of what it could do.

"That's amazing!!! Can you invent any kind of sword you want?" I asked.

"I can, but skill level and MP pose some restrictions on it."

"Still, that's an incredible skill."

"Th-thank you," she stammered. I just said what I thought, but Rei's face turned red, as if praise embarrassed her.

"You're amazing yourself, Rin," she added quickly. "Kazami-san said you were weak, but he *was* lying. If he'd been telling the truth, you couldn't have moved like that."

"Oh, uh, really? Thanks." It was my turn to be embarrassed. What was this vibe we had going?

Wait, this wasn't the time for friendly conversation!

"Did you notice that the orcs were stronger than usual?" I asked.

"Yes, I got that impression."

"I used Appraisal on one, and it was level 600. Orcs should be around level 400 on this floor. It's bizarre that they'd be on par with the dungeon boss. Maybe we should try to figure out why?"

"Do you have any ideas?"

"A few..."

A dungeon's resident monsters could grow stronger for numerous reasons. The problem was determining which one reason it could be.

The dungeon itself wasn't vibrating, so it couldn't have been the *worst* possible reason. If it were, we would be in serious trouble. Whatever the cause, I wanted to stop this problem before it got more out of hand.

"I want to investigate the area. How about you? Want to return to the surface?" I asked.

Rei shook her head. "No, but I'll go with you."

I hesitated, but eventually conceded.

"Okay. Let's go."

Rei and I began our search on the fifth floor. Unexpectedly, we found the cause almost immediately. As we walked, an enormous space opened up along our path where several monster corpses lay. A group of orcs were devouring them.

"Monster cannibalism," I said, surveying the scene.

Rei tilted her head. "Monster cannibalism...?"

"Yeah. Normally, the dungeon absorbs monsters once they're defeated. But if no one removes the magic stones, sometimes they don't absorb them. Other monsters eat the corpses, which makes them stronger. The orcs we just fought probably came from here."

"Which means we'll solve the issue if we defeat every orc here?"

"Exactly. I want to make sure no other adventurers run into any unexpected trouble."

"Leave it to me."

Rei was going to help? I'd barely blinked before Rei swung her magic sword. The blade extended and severed the necks of the nearest three orcs, sending the heads soaring. The eyes goggled at us.

"How was that?" Rei asked with a smug face.

"Definitely effective, although I wish I could've checked their stats first." Not that I was unhappy to see three orcs go down before the battle even began.

"Wanna tackle the rest?" I asked.

"Sure."

Rei and I charged toward the overpowered horde of feasting orcs together.

◆❦◆

"That's the last of them," I said.

With the throng of orcs defeated, I cut the magic stone from the dead one laying at my feet. Rei activated a fire version of her magic sword and burned the pile of bodies from before we arrived. Magic stones were all that remained once the corpses burnt to nothing. Taking resources from monsters we didn't kill felt like cheating, but there they were.

Problem solved. I had to hand it to Rei: she was a huge help. I was incredibly grateful.

"Thank you, Rei. Couldn't have done it without you."

"It was a team effort. If not for your knowledge, I couldn't have handled this either."

"A team effort? Yeah, you're right." *We got through it together.* Maybe it was okay to let myself think that way.

Rei parted her lips. I waited.

"Listen, Rin. I want to ask you something."

"What is it?"

Her serious expression turned my mood serious as well. Once she gathered her thoughts, she spoke.

"Why are you working as an adventurer?"

"*Why...?*"

That wasn't the question I expected, so it threw me off guard. I wondered what use she could have for my answer, but I supposed it didn't really matter.

My reason for becoming an adventurer was something I had only shared with Hana, and something I never intended to tell anyone else. It was kind of embarrassing, after all. But after spending the day with Rei, I'd fostered a kinship with her. It was strangely easy to trust her.

"When I was younger, an adventurer saved my life."

I told her the full story: how a brave adventurer had dived in to rescue me, and that I now aspired to be like the man who stood between me and certain death. Rei's expression deepened as she listened.

"I see. So that's why I'm so drawn to..." she murmured.

"Hm? Did you say my name?" I asked.

"No, it's nothing. Do you remember the name of the adventurer who saved you?"

"No, he quickly left to drive off the remaining monsters. I never learned his name. He was strong, so I don't doubt he's a first-rate adventurer these days."

What *was* he doing nowadays? I wouldn't be surprised if he'd retired in the intervening years.

"Thanks, Rin. I'm glad I heard your story."

"Oh, sure. Glad you're glad," I said awkwardly. I didn't think my story was that entertaining, but if she was satisfied, then it was worth telling.

It was about time we moved on.

"Rei, what're your plans after this? Still going to dungeon dive?" I asked.

"Yeah. I want to fight a little longer."

Rei and I spent another hour defeating the dungeon's monsters together. I always fought solo, but it was nice battling alongside a fellow adventurer. Who knew?

◆⌃◆

That evening, Rei showered while she replayed the day's events in her head. The center of her thoughts? The boy she'd traveled the dungeon with—Amane Rin.

She was very interested in him.

Kazami was the one who put him on her radar. He'd said Rin was a member of the Kings of Unique but left the party because his unique skill was useless. He also said Rin was still dungeon diving every day since he realized his adventurer potential was essentially null and void.

Rei had doubted the story. After all, why would an adventurer with no future persevere? Adventurers had lots of reasons for doing what they did—rank, money, fame, privilege, prestige—which meant *many* held high ambitions. That was why someone publicly slapped with the label *useless* would shy away from ridicule and quit. Even Rei, a new adventurer, understood that was how the world worked.

At the time she heard the story, her interest in Rin was minimal. It only increased a few months later, when she met him at Kenzaki Dungeon. She wasn't the best conversationalist, but when she remembered his story, she worked up the nerve to talk to him.

Amane Rin surprised her with the unwavering willpower in his gaze.

She believed a person's true colors were revealed when they were backed into a corner. When things were good, it was easy to be kind. It was during a crisis that a person who claimed a sense of justice may reveal their true self-interested nature. They could do something terrible. Even if they didn't, they might put up dark walls in the aftermath and become consumed by negative emotions.

But Rin was different: he had an openness about him, confident yet genuine. And today, Rei realized why.

He wasn't after status, celebrity, or wealth. He simply wanted the strength to protect other people, like the man who'd saved his life.

I see now. That's the reason Rin never became disheartened.

What he truly wanted wasn't something that recognition could give.

Interestingly, Rei shared a common interest with him. She'd dodged Rin's question about her hobbies, but she too liked manga and anime. Anything fiction-related, actually. Fantasies with cool heroes who always saved the day were her favorite. Since she was little, she'd admired those kinds of stories the most. She wanted to become the hero who gallantly came to the rescue in the nick of time.

Rei didn't want to be protected. Unlike some girls of her generation, she wanted to be the protector instead. She knew her stance was unusual, but she understood the truth: for anyone living in this day and age, fantasy was no longer fiction. In a dungeon, gender had no bearing on success.

It was an opportunity for anyone to become a hero.

Unlike Rin, she didn't have a dramatic origin story for her dream. However, they most certainly shared the same one.

"I want to talk to him again." Her heart thumped.

As she turned the shower handle and stopped the water, Rei thought of the boy who shared her dream. She'd listened to his life story, but she hadn't shared anything about herself. Next time they met, she wanted to tell him about herself—including her favorite anime series.

Rin was the first person she'd ever felt this way about.

"How strange, when we've only just met..."

After just one day fighting together, it felt like they existed on the same wavelength. Kurosaki Rei would be thrilled to become his friend.

CHAPTER 6

DISCUSSIONS AND REUNIONS

THE NEXT DAY, I decided to trek through Kenzaki again.

"I'll use the Kirikuji Short Sword on my way to the bottom floor, then switch to Nameless for the boss. Yeah, better get going!"

I activated Dungeon Teleportation and warped through the floors. Each time a monster appeared at my landing point, I efficiently exterminated it. Orcs and horned rabbits went down in one hit; red boars died with three quick slashes.

"Just a month ago, taking down level 400 monsters was a distant dream," I said to myself, the emotions hitting me after a fight. Despite my growth, I wasn't yet satisfied with my strength. I hurried toward the last floor.

Due to fighting off monsters and harvesting materials, thirty minutes passed before I reached the last floor, where I swapped to Nameless and battled the high orc. This was my third time, so the boss fight was familiar. I defeated it without taking a single hit.

"You have defeated the dungeon boss."

"Gained XP: Level increased by 1!"

"Dungeon Takedown Reward: Level increased by 20!"

As usual, the dungeon takedown rewards were a level up and an Exploding Stone.

"Nice. How much SP have I gained so far?"

I opened my stats display, which showed 410 SP, then checked my current skills. Time to form a new strategy.

"It really is better to hold off on leveling up Dungeon Teleportation and invest in battle skills for now."

There was no reason to boost Dungeon Teleportation from LV 11 to LV 12 beyond optimizing MP cost. The current cost didn't hold me back. Besides, it wasn't a battle skill. The better option was to use SP on active skills.

Boosting both Herculean Strength and High-speed Movement to LV 10 was my first objective. I wanted to obtain new skills too—namely, Enemy Detection, Evasion, and Status Condition Resistance. The dungeons I planned to visit in the near future would have places where physical strength wasn't enough. I needed to prepare for all manner of tricky situations.

"If I obtain abilities for a variety of dungeons, that'll make for effective leveling. I can spec into Dungeon Teleportation after that."

Once I had my plan and reentered to the Return Zone, I faced Kenzaki again. In one day, I beat the dungeon fifteen times, gained 301 levels, and earned three million yen.

Again, I went to Kenzaki for a day of speed leveling. I ignored the monsters that spawned on my path and targeted the profitable red boars. Using Nameless, I beheaded them and stored the corpses in my Item Box. They remained in peak condition for maximum resale value inside it. Once I filled my Item Box to capacity and harvested the takedown reward from the high orc, I would earn a pretty penny.

"Money makes the world go 'round. Gotta get it where I can."

My top priority was leveling up, but I couldn't forget to feed my wallet. I kept that thought in the back of my mind as I continued.

"Haaa!"

I swung Nameless and defeated the high orc for the twentieth time that day. Now that I'd surpassed level 1,200, the weapon didn't weigh me down. Defeating the high orc was a piece of cake.

The system dinged in my head.

"Dungeon Takedown Reward: Level increased by 20."

"Yes! That's what I'm talking about."

I collected the Exploding Stone then harvested the magic stone from the high orc's body. Sadly, I didn't have space for it in my Item Box.

"Max capacity, huh? Right when I boosted it to LV 4... Oh well! Might as well call it a day. It's late."

After that, I sold the day's spoils, the Exploding Stone excluded. The day's haul was four hundred levels and 4 million yen.

The day after, I continued my usual routine at Kenzaki.

I stepped into battle with the high orc for the twenty-third time that day. Just days ago, this boss's strength invoked shock and fear in me. But now?

"These strikes hit lightly."

The high orc sprinted toward me with its giant club, its monstrous strength focused on crushing me. I deflected it with ease.

"Take this!" I shouted and swung Nameless with my right hand. That was all it took to cut the high orc in half. The top half of its body hit the ground with a thump.

"Dungeon Takedown Reward: Level increased by 20!"

The system's second chime marked the moment I'd waited for.

"You have reached this dungeon's maximum number of allotted victories."

"Bonus Reward: Level increased by 50."

"You will no longer receive rewards for defeating this dungeon."

"Yes! I added Kenzaki to my title!"

It took sixty runs, but I completed it. Yumemi, Shion, and now Kenzaki—a third dungeon to add to my Dungeon Traveler title.

"I gained a nice chunk of SP too."

With my attention on the looping dungeon, I'd racked up 11,510 SP. I checked my skills and considered how to spend it.

OBTAINED SKILLS

Herculean Strength LV 6 → LV 7 (SP NEEDED: 700)

High-speed Movement LV 4 → LV 5 (SP NEEDED: 500)

Item Box LV 4 → LV 5 (SP NEEDED: 1,000)

NEW SKILLS

Enemy Detection LV 1 (SP NEEDED: 100)

Evasion LV 1 (SP NEEDED: 100)

Status Condition Resistance LV 1 (SP NEEDED: 100)

"I've invested enough in Item Box for the time being, so I should prioritize Herculean Strength and High-speed Movement..."

I tried some mental calculations. Herculean Strength required 3,400 SP to reach LV 10 and High-speed Movement required 4,500 SP to reach LV 10. That totaled 7,900 SP, with plenty left over for other skills.

"If that's the case, those two boosts are a must."

If I used 3,000 of the remaining 3,610 SP to raise Enemy Detection, Evasion, and Status Condition Resistance to LV 4 each, I'd be left with 610 SP. Quite the skill improvement. No matter how I changed moving forward, these skills would definitely help me along.

"That settles it."

I confidently allotted my SP to some skills:

> **HERCULEAN STRENGTH LV MAX:** Attack +3,000
>
> **HIGH-SPEED MOVEMENT LV MAX:** Speed +3,000
>
> **ENEMY DETECTION LV 4:** Uses MP to detect the presence of nearby humans and monsters.
>
> **EVASION LV 4:** Uses MP to erase the user's presence from the perception of nearby humans and monsters.
>
> **STATUS CONDITION RESISTANCE LV 4:** Provides resistance to status conditions such as poison, paralysis, and sleep.

"Nice, nice, looking good."

Just a few seconds scored me a *massive* power boost. I wanted to boost Enemy Detection, Evasion, and Status Condition Resistance to LV 10 but would manage that later.

"Back to the drawing board, then. Starting tomorrow, I'll grind another dungeon."

I was under the Span from beating Kenzaki Dungeon, so I had to choose a dungeon from my past to dive into. Out of the dungeons I'd tackled, Yunagi Dungeon and Arikawa Dungeon (an E-rank dungeon from my earliest adventurer days) were the only ones I hadn't added to my Dungeon Traveler title. I decided to fix that, starting with Yunagi.

Three days later, I was done.

"You have reached this dungeon's maximum number of allotted victories."

"Bonus Reward: Level increased by 15."

"You will no longer receive rewards for defeating this dungeon."

I maxed out my rewards from Yunagi without issue, which filled four out of the ten slots for my Dungeon Traveler title. That night, I delegated the SP I'd amassed to the skills I needed. That was when Yui contacted me out of the blue.

The next day, I went to a mall in the city center to meet up with Yui. I arrived earlier than our scheduled time, but she arrived a bit late.

"Oh! Rin-senpai! Sorry, did I make you wait?"

"Yeah."

"Hey! You're supposed to say, 'No, not at all' or something to make me feel better!"

Was I? I'd never gone out to meet any girls before, so I didn't know.

"I'm kidding," she said. "Thanks for meeting me today. Why don't we find a café and sit?"

I agreed, and we entered a nearby café. She ordered a sweet-looking drink with whipped cream on top. Still regretting that black coffee from last time we met up, I ordered a milk tea. No human being deserved to suffer the bitter monstrosity that was black coffee.

Once we had our first sips of our drinks, I spoke up. "So, what kind of advice did you need? If you're asking me, it's gotta be about dungeons, right?"

"Ding ding ding! You're right! I'm not close with any

adventurers, but I did think of you." She sipped her drink before continuing. "So, the other day, I received a guild invitation."

"Oh yeah?"

Adventurer guilds were exactly as you'd expect: organizations where adventurers gathered and worked together. Unlike parties, they required a minimum of ten members. The biggest ones had over one hundred adventurers to their name. Guilds with the most powerful adventurers secured government-granted privileges that were otherwise unheard of for civilian organizations. Guilds watched the adventurer marketplace like hawks circling prey and swooped in to scoop up top adventurers to join their ranks.

Guilds wanted to recruit talented members, and adventurers wanted to join influential guilds. For adventurers, guilds could provide countless advantages. Senior members had veterans' knowledge to offer, all members gained access to the most valuable materials, and it was easy to form a party. Those were just a few of the immediate ones.

Some adventurers didn't like operating under a commanding body, though, so they didn't join a guild. Kazami and the others fell under that umbrella.

"By the way, Yui, how much have you leveled up since we last met?"

"I broke level 100 yesterday!"

"And you received an invitation already? That's amazing!" I said quietly, genuinely surprised.

There were the big guilds and then there were small to mid-sized guilds. Whether they had the time or resources to train up a low-level adventurer was the clincher. With the right setup, any adventurer, regardless of talent, could build their strength to a certain point.

For example, someone who dove once per week for five years would end up a higher level than someone who spent a year in danger but pushed through. Financially speaking, small to midsize guilds would want the firepower of the former, not the latter. Only a guild with lots of funding would invest money and resources into a talented-but-green adventurer. At level 100, Yui was definitely one of those.

"Can I ask the name of the guild that invited you?" I asked.

"They're named Yoizuki."

"Yoizuki...?"

"Yes. This is the card they gave me when they invited me."

The name rang a bell, but I couldn't pin it. Besides the guild name, the card displayed a moon and sword motif—the guild's emblem. I uttered a small sound of recognition.

"I remember now. They became a nationally ranked guild after just a few years."

"Yes, the guild said the same thing! They sang their own praises and recommended joining because it has lots of room to grow. They want me because healers are so rare."

"I bet they would."

Health recovery potions were expensive precisely because healers were incredibly hard to come by. Even *with* potions, healers were necessary, and some healers could offer support magic on top of healing magic. One healer could enable an entire party to handle a range of situations, which meant guilds were desperate to acquire them.

After hearing all that, I had a general sense for what advice Yui needed.

"You want to ask me whether or not it's worth joining this guild?" I asked.

"Yes, that's right!"

"I'm not versed in the nitty-gritty though. That okay?"

Yui leaned over the table and nodded vigorously. "Of course!"

Whoa, she was close.

"*Ahem.* The scout might've mentioned what I'm about to say, but I'll explain the pros and cons of joining a guild."

"Please do!" she said enthusiastically.

"First, the pros. The top one would probably be support. Big guilds can provide equipment and dungeon information. The work you've had to do to get your equipment can be done for you. That's no small thing."

I swallowed a mouthful of my milk tea.

"Another upside is that guilds will pick members from their ranks that complement your abilities and form a party for you. That way, you won't form a party with untrustworthy people. You know how important *that* is, don't you?"

"Yes..." Yui ducked her head. Hearing that must have brought her back to the time we met—back when her party left her to die.

"Next, there's the cons, which have to do with restricting your freedoms."

"They have restrictions?"

"Yeah. If you become a member, you have to schedule your dives. That usually happens for parties anyway, but the problem is the Dungeon Association's demands."

Yui sat upright. "Oh, I've heard a bit about that. Guilds must meet certain requirements in exchange for their special privileges, right?"

"Yeah, you've got the shape of it. The Dungeon Association can call on guilds to handle strange occurrences involving dungeons. Unless there's extenuating circumstances, members have to come when called on, potentially putting them in danger. Or so I hear."

I'd never actually seen that happen, but it was a famous hot topic and a dealbreaker for a lot of adventurers.

"All things considered, if you want to get stronger quickly, a guild is a solid option. But if you value freedom and your own schedule, I think it's better to go your own way. Why did you become an adventurer, anyway?"

"The reason I started, you mean?"

"Yeah. Not a lot of people work as adventurers during high school, so I'm curious. If you don't want to tell me, you don't have to."

After a short pause, Yui spoke. "At first, I didn't plan to do it. I was afraid of fighting monsters and holding a weapon felt so weird and uncomfortable. I figured, if I got stats, that'd make my body more durable, and I could leave it at that."

True. Lots of people sought out stats so they could survive things like traffic accidents. Most people, actually. Only a fraction of them dedicated themselves to the life-threatening work of an adventurer. Yui was originally one of the former, but it sounded like her story diverged from there.

"Once I got my stats and realized I had healer abilities, it gave me an idea. I was afraid to fight monsters on the front lines, but I *could* support others from behind. That's why I'm still doing it. It feels worthwhile."

Yui gazed at the palms of her hands.

"Maybe it was a coincidence I awakened this ability, but I see a purpose in it. What I want most is to develop the power to save people's lives. I want to *make* it develop." She looked up at me with determined eyes.

"Sounds like you've made your decision," I said.

"I have. I'll be courageous and join the guild."

"Yeah? Well, you can always quit if it doesn't work out. Your life is the most important thing in all this, so be careful that no one takes advantage of your skills."

I said it with a smile. Yui matched it with her own.

"No worries on that front! When I told them I was still in high school, they said I only need to participate on my days off. They'll pay me more than normal healers too. I could beat your earnings soon!"

"You talk a big game."

Maybe she would've a while ago, but now, I had made more than ten million yen in one day. Could she beat that? I felt competitive enough to fire that back, but I kept my mouth shut instead.

We talked a little more, then stood to leave the café. I went to pay, but Yui interrupted me.

"Wait, Rin-senpai! You gave me advice, so I'll pay."

"Don't worry about it. Besides, you won't receive your first payment from the guild for a while. If you want to pay it forward, how about picking up the bill another time?"

"Rin-senpai..."

Yui went still and stared at me. Finally, she seemed to view me as a guy who could handle himself. Then she said something unexpected.

"If you're so considerate, kind, and reliable...why have you never had a girlfriend?"

"Hold up. Are you making fun of me? How do you even know that? You stalking me or something?"

"N-no! Hana-chan told me while we were texting!"

"Why were you even talking about that?!" I would have to lecture Hana once I got home.

I left the café thoroughly ruffled.

On the way toward the mall's exit, I spotted a familiar figure wearing headphones, standing at the corner of the CD shop. A *very* familiar girl at this point. To my surprise, Yui spoke up before I could.

"Oh? Kurosaki-san?"

The girl—Kurosaki Rei—jumped and turned our way. She had fear in her eyes.

"Um, Rin?"

"Hey. Long time no see."

"Right."

About a week had passed since we trekked Kenzaki together. Seeing us greet each other, Yui interjected.

"Wait one second here! I'm the one who called your name, but you responded to *him*?"

"Who are you, exactly?" Rei asked.

"Don't you recognize me?! We're in the same class. I'm Kasai Yui!"

"Now that you mention it, I think I remember you."

Huh. Yui and Rei were classmates. It didn't sound like they spoke often.

"Rin-senpai, how do you even know Rei?" Yui asked.

"She's an adventurer too. We met outside a dungeon."

"Really? I had no idea!" Yui looked genuinely surprised.

While Yui and I spoke, Rei attempted to slide a CD back onto the shelf. Unfortunately for her, I didn't miss it. The CD's jacket had colorful character art of some girls on it, which meant it was an anime soundtrack. At that moment, I understood. We were kindred spirits.

It was likely she'd hid the CD because she was afraid we would ask her about it. Could embarrassment be the reason she kept her hobbies a secret when I asked last week? I pretended not to notice.

Yui spoke up.

"I never expected to run into you in a place like this. I'm glad to really talk to you for the first time. You always listen to music with your headphones on during breaks, so I didn't think I should bother you—wait! That drawing of a cute girl must mean that's from an anime, right?"

Stop it, Yui. That attack is super effective on people like us!

Rei floundered for words but found none. Her face bloomed bright red now that she was under Yui's microscope. I doubted Yui had ill intentions, but anyone would feel embarrassed when put on the spot. In that regard, I could relate to Rei.

I faked a cough and changed the subject. "Got any plans to dungeon dive today, Rei?"

She grabbed the escape rope I gave her. "Y-yeah, I'm going to meet up with Kazami and the others and go to Kenzaki."

"I had no idea this many anime soundtracks existed..."

Yikes. I tried so hard to steer the conversation away, but Yui swerved it right back. She was closely inspecting the anime soundtrack section. Had she heard a word we said? If she hadn't, there was no need to answer her.

I faced Rei beside me to find her staring, just like the first time we met. The silence stretched between us until I spoke.

"What's the matter?"

"Nothing. Are *you* going to a dungeon today?" Rei asked.

"No. I fulfilled my Dungeon Trav—*ahem*. I *beat* a dungeon yesterday, so I'm taking the day to recharge."

That was close. I nearly let my unusual title slip. Fortunately, I deflected, or so I thought.

"Rei?" She gazed into the middle distance, as if mulling something over. Did she suspect me?

"If you're with Yui on your day off," she said slowly, "are you two in a *relationship*?"

"What?" Rei had gotten the completely wrong idea. "No, not at all. She asked me to meet up and give her advice as a fellow adventurer. That's the extent of it."

"Oh. I guess that makes sense."

I let out a breath of relief. Thank goodness she believed me.

"Do you like younger girls?"

Where had her thoughts run off to? What was the correct answer to that question? Did she have doubts about my relationship with Yui? She seemed convinced a few seconds ago! My instincts shouted that I needed to answer carefully. If I spoke vaguely about Yui, Rei could still misinterpret my answer. An image of Hana's smirk formed in the back of my mind.

Yeah, I needed to man up and answer honestly.

"If I had to say whether I like or dislike Yui, sure, I do like her."

"Oh, you like her? Ah..."

Rei blanched and looked away. Great, that was definitely the wrong answer. Nevertheless, I didn't want to lie to her, so I had no regrets.

"Rin-senpai, what are you two talking about?" Yui asked as she pulled her head out of the clouds and turned away from the anime soundtrack section and got back into the conversation.

"Small talk, it's nothing important." Thank *goodness* Yui could change the topic.

Right as I thought that, the entire mall began to shudder.

"What's happening?!" Yui cried.

"Maybe an earthquake?"

At least, that was my guess, but the emergency alert displayed on the TV monitors throughout the mall proved me wrong. The volume on them was silent, which only made my nervousness mount.

"Emergency. Emergency. Kenzaki Dungeon is subject to a dungeon collapse. Civilians must evacuate. Requesting assistance from all adventurers C-rank or above."

"What—A dungeon collapse?!" I shouted.

"Rin-san, a dungeon collapse means..."

"This is going to get ugly real quick."

Yui and Rei's faces were strained. As adventurers, they knew exactly the danger that was coming.

A dungeon collapse was a rare phenomenon where a dungeon self-destructed. Usually only adventurers could travel through the Gate, but during a collapse, monsters could too.

That meant one thing.

"Monsters are about to swarm the city."

CHAPTER 7

DUNGEON COLLAPSE

FTER THE DUNGEON COLLAPSE began, all C-rank or above adventurers were called to assist. Without hesitation, I responded to the call.

"Rei, I'm going to go defeat the monsters outside. What about you?" I asked.

"I'm going too, obviously." Her eyes were unwavering.

"Wait, Rin-senpai! I'll go too!" Yui blurted, right before we set out.

"Are you familiar with Kenzaki's difficulty level? You need to be level 500 at a minimum, and with the dungeon collapse, these monsters could be stronger and more brutal than usual."

"I wouldn't fight. I want to use my magic to heal anyone who gets hurt from a monster encounter. But, if you think I'll get in the way, I won't come."

"Hmm..."

Yui had a good argument, which made me rethink things. People without stats couldn't use health recovery potions, but healing magic worked *on* them. Healers were scarce, and one more person with superior abilities on deck could shift the winds in our favor. Besides, wasn't helping people the reason she stayed an adventurer? I wanted to respect her purpose.

"Okay, Yui, you're in. Just stay close to us."

"I will! Thank you so much!" She beamed and nodded.

Worst case scenario, I could protect her so long as she remained within ten meters of us. Beating Kenzaki sixty times gave me the confidence to make that assessment.

We left the mall and stepped outside, where I realized we still wore our casual clothes.

"If the monsters are surfacing, we should change our outfits before they get here," I said.

Rei nodded. "Good point."

A soft glow surrounded me and Rei. Courtesy of our Item Box skill, the glow quick-changed us into our adventurer equipment. I'd usually use this upon entering or exiting a dungeon, so this was my first time using it in the city.

Yui pouted at us. "I don't have Item Box. I feel like an outsider."

"You have to admit, you look funny as the only one dressed like that," I said.

"Now you're just being a bully!"

"My bad, my bad," I said with a laugh. "I won't put you in a position where you have to fight. Don't worry."

"Oh, well," she giggled. "In that case, I forgive you!"

Suddenly, a ringtone pierced through our banter. It was Rei's cell phone.

"Sorry, I need to take this," she said.

"Sure."

Was it someone with an opinion on whether she should join in on the emergency summons? She exchanged a few words with the caller then returned to us, not quite making eye contact.

"Who was it?" I asked.

"Kazami-san. He told me to meet the party before I join in on the fray."

"Oh."

Kazami-san and the rest of them were in the area. In that case, it would be easier for Rei to fight with her party members.

"Sorry, but I need to bow out," she apologized.

"I understand. We're gonna go on ahead. But...take care of yourself, Rei."

"I will. You two be careful too."

With those parting words, she left for the rendezvous with Kazami and his party. Watching her leave made my chest tighten with unease, but why?

"I must be imagining things," I said to myself.

"Rin-senpai? Did you say something?" Yui asked.

"Nothing. Let's hurry."

"Okay!"

Yui and I set out for Kenzaki Dungeon together. We were a few minutes along—still only a third of the way to the dungeon—when we encountered our first monster.

"There's a monster here!" someone yelled. "Are any adventurers nearby?!"

I turned toward the shout, where a single male adventurer was fighting three orcs at once. An injured person lay collapsed behind him.

"Rin-senpai!"

"I know."

I quickly surveyed the area, and once I confirmed there weren't other monsters around, I charged the orcs in an eruption of speed. They'd worked together to corner the man, but I slipped past their defenses and cut their sides. In a spray of blood, the three orcs crumpled like paper.

"Huh...?" The adventurer blinked at me with shock.

"Are you okay?"

"Y-yeah. Was that you? You moved so fast I couldn't see it."

"That was me. I'm glad I made it in time."

Yui caught up and cast her healing magic over the injured civilian.

"Wow. My wound is healing..."

"Thank you. You *seriously* saved us."

No one in the area seemed severely injured, and healing the person went off without a hitch. Ignoring whether the injury was severe or not, it amazed me how quickly Yui's low-level healing magic worked. I had just glimpsed how talented she would become as a healer.

Once she was finished, she returned to my side. "I'm done. Should we keep going to Kenzaki?"

"Hmm..."

I thought it over for a minute. That was the plan, but if

monsters were already so far from the dungeon, there might be a better approach. We *could* go to Kenzaki, but that didn't mean we'd necessarily make a difference.

Dungeon collapses consisted of a few nasty features. First, hordes of monsters flowed from the Gate. Second, the monsters lurking inside the dungeon increased in strength. Theoretically, the second feature occurred because a collapse released the mana that held a dungeon together. Because of that, the monsters absorbed the mana and doubled their strength. The dungeon boss would power up even more as well. In such an amplified state, it was called a *final boss*.

Defeating a final boss completely destroyed the stability of a dungeon and completed its collapse. But the longer it took, the stronger the final boss became. If the dungeon collapsed before the final boss was defeated, the last boss would ascend to the surface.

Adventurers *had* to defeat the final boss as soon as possible, but thanks to its tremendous strength, only a party a rank above the collapsing dungeon could hope to quash the threat.

Kenzaki was a C-rank dungeon: that meant we needed a B-rank party with adventurers averaging around level 5,000 to defeat the final boss. It stung to admit, but I wasn't there yet.

I also had another reason *not* to pursue the final boss. I told Rei that I'd beaten a dungeon yesterday. A collapse would let monsters leave the dungeon, but anyone subject to a Span shouldn't be allowed to enter it. To maintain my cover, I wanted to avoid entering Kenzaki at all costs. Instead, I would put my effort into acting as a support.

I answered Yui with my decision. "Let's focus on exterminating the monsters leaving Kenzaki and healing the injured."

"Got it!" She nodded without a shred of doubt.

We stayed above ground to clean up the mess—and hoped for the best.

Meanwhile, Rei arrived at Kenzaki with the Kings of Unique. Outside the dungeon, a crowd of adventurers was engaged in nervous chatter.

"Seriously, the guild-appointed B-rank party won't be here for another twenty or thirty minutes?"

"Yeah. Collapsing dungeons are totally chaotic, so it's taking them a while to prepare for all the possibilities."

"I get that they can't summon adventurers under a Span, but at this rate, the final boss will only get stronger!"

Based on what she heard, Rei gathered that they would have to wait a while longer before the adventurers chosen to defeat the final boss arrived. Nervousness rippled through the crowd. At worst, the reinforcements wouldn't prevent the final boss from growing to maximum strength and storming the surface.

A voice rang out over the anxious crowd.

"Ha ha *ha*! This sure looks like trouble, but no need to worry! The Kings of Unique have arrived!"

Rei startled. The voice came from Kazami beside her.

"What...?" she asked. His abrupt proclamation filled her

with apprehension. Around them, people's reactions were the complete opposite.

"Wow! The Kings of Unique! Maybe they can do something about the collapse."

"Yeah! We don't need to wait for the B-rank party!"

Kazami's smile widened, their words bolstering his mood. "That's right! No waiting necessary. We're going to wipe out the final boss ourselves!"

Rei stood frozen, unsure what to do. After countless dungeon dives with her party, she knew what they were capable of—and Kazami wasn't wrong. Their power *could* be enough to defeat the final boss. But the fact remained that the B-rank party hadn't arrived yet, and a dungeon during a collapse was unpredictable. The safest choice was to wait. If they *really* couldn't, they should find some other way to help.

Before she could speak up, a dungeon supervisor hurried up to them. Her expression was panicked.

"Please, wait! A dungeon under collapse is extremely dangerous and erratic. I'm sorry, but do you have experience facing B-rank dungeons?"

"No, but I don't think that's an issue," Kazami replied breezily. "We're *unique* skill holders, and all but one of us are above level 2,000. A little extra power won't make this dungeon's monsters a match for us."

"I concede that you might be capable of defeating the final boss, but you can't guarantee that," the dungeon supervisor countered. "The final boss could be ten times stronger than usual.

If you insist on entering, would you *please* wait until the B-rank party arrives?"

"You sure are stubborn. Now's the time to attack! What if the dungeon completely collapses and the final boss surfaces while we're twiddling our thumbs? You want the blame for that?"

"I...I..." The dungeon supervisor stammered. After some hesitation, she offered an alternative plan. "Okay, how about this? Instead of challenging the final boss, why don't you clear the path to the boss room?"

"Clear the path?" Kazami questioned.

"Correct. If monsters swarm the B-rank party, that'll cost them time and energy. If you go first, you can clear the path for them. The normal monsters you encounter should only be about two times stronger, and if your stats are what you say they are, they should be no problem for you to handle. If you have stamina left over, will you assist the B-rank party with the final boss?"

Rei considered that perfectly reasonable. She imagined Kazami would too.

"Hmm, can't say I'm completely happy about it, but that's not a bad compromise," he said. "Fine, we'll agree to your plan."

"Thank you. Do any of your party members have a telepathic skill? Transmission devices won't work, and if something goes wrong, I'd like you to be able to contact me."

"Unfortunately not, but don't worry! I highly doubt we'll need that. Now, why don't we wrap up the preamble, hmm?"

Kazami smirked and glanced at the other party members. "You heard the plan. We're going in. Sakura, Yuuya, Kosuke, hop to it." He looked to Rei last. "You too, Rei."

Rei said nothing. Slowly, she followed them down the stairs to the Return Zone, where misgivings prodded at the back of her mind.

She was the lowest level party member—she might hold them back somehow.

No... I'll be okay.

She decided she could do it. If the dungeon supervisor was correct, the monsters would be double their usual strength at most. That amounted to level 1,000. Rei had recently surpassed level 600, and thanks to her unique skill, she could handle two or three monsters on her own. More than ten would change the game, but she had Kazami and the others with her. Their help put her in much *less* danger.

Besides, Rei sincerely hoped her efforts could save people.

While not long had passed since she became an adventurer, Rei's dream to become a hero was long-held and treasured. She may not have the power to realize her dream yet, but she did have the power to assist her party.

In front of the Gate, Rei took a steadying breath. She was a member of a party, and she would do everything she could to assist them.

Steadfastly, she stepped through the Gate.

About thirty minutes had passed since the Kings of Unique entered Kenzaki Dungeon. They were descending toward the last floor in a chaotic flurry when five red boars appeared in their path.

"Sakura, what's the Appraisal?" Kazami asked.

"All five are level 800. Nothing to worry about."

"Sounds about right. Lightning Strike!"

Lightning shot from Kazami's fingers, instantly burning the three red boars in the center to a crisp. Rei and the others followed through the path he'd paved forward while ignoring the other two red boars.

They'd progressed well, but something bothered Rei.

"We haven't cleared every monster. Are you sure this is enough, Kazami?"

Numbers wouldn't matter if the goal was reaching the end of the dungeon, but to Rei, it didn't seem like they were doing enough to clear the way for the B-rank party.

Kazami nodded confidently. "Of *course* it's enough. Think about it. This is *a B-rank* party, remember? Any monster we can kill instantly is a monster that's even easier for them."

Rei hesitated. "...Right."

Kazami's answer didn't fully put her concerns to rest, but there *was* some logic to it. She decided to accept his explanation as it was.

They defeated more monsters while deflecting others. The deeper they went, the more monsters they left behind. Rei asked the same question again partway through, but Kazami didn't listen—and she didn't push. After fifty minutes had passed, Rei and the rest of the party arrived at the door to the boss room.

We arrived much faster than I expected. Rei took a deep breath. Now, they would wait for the B-rank party, or so she thought.

"You know what?" Kazami said abruptly. "I don't think *dungeon collapses* are as big a deal as they say."

Doubt sunk into Rei. What was he implying? She didn't wonder too long, because he continued and said something unbelievable.

"I say we challenge the final boss ourselves. What do you think?"

"What?"

Rei widened her eyes in disbelief. Sakura, the other female member who joined long before Rei, gave him a stern look.

"Shin, what are you trying to do? Weren't we going to wait for reinforcements?"

"I changed my mind! That was the plan, until I realized that monsters influenced by a dungeon collapse aren't as strong as they say. We can take down the final boss ourselves, no prob." No one responded, so Kazami continued. "Come on. Isn't it about time we won some prestige for ourselves?"

"Prestige?"

"Think about it. On paper, we're C-rank adventurers. If we defeat a final boss a B-rank party was supposed to handle, that would show everyone how powerful we really are. This is an opportunity for getting recognition!"

Rei understood Kazami's point, but he was practically admitting that he was only in this to make a name for himself. Didn't anyone else see that? She turned to the others, hopeful they'd see past his selfish desires.

They betrayed her.

"Maybe Shin's right," Sakura replied. "Currently, the only thing notable about our party is our unique skills. If we make our mark here, we'll enhance our reputation even further."

"Exactly! And the boss is a *high orc*. My Fortress skill will render any boosted attack power useless," Yuuya added.

"Let's hit it!" Kousuke chimed in.

Sakura, Yuuya, and Kousuke agreed. At this rate, the five of them—including Rei—were going to challenge the final boss, but she desperately wanted to stop them.

"Hold on. Are we seriously going in?" she asked.

"Obviously. Don't let your lower level worry you. You can stand back while we take care of the boss ourselves," Kazami assured her.

"But that's not what we promised the dungeon supervisor!" Rei objected.

"That won't matter once we beat the boss. I don't get why you're opposed. Stand back, collect the dungeon takedown rewards, and bask in the glory that's bound to come! Just be happy about it, Rei."

Casting her eyes across the faces of the other party members, she finally understood how she differed from them.

She prioritized ending the collapse and preventing more damage outside the dungeon. Kazami and the rest of the party thought the situation provided a convenient way to show off.

Saving lives and preventing damage were a mere afterthought to them.

"I'm the *leader*, and this is my decision," Kazami said. "The majority agree with me. If you insist on hanging back, you can wait here by yourself. That is, if you think you can fight off the monsters alone."

That was why Rei had never liked him: Kazami said condescending crap like that so, so easily. Her hands curled into tight fists as she remembered something crucial:

A person shows their true colors when they're backed into a corner.

That wasn't the only time people revealed their true selves. They also did it when they had the chance to gain money and status. For Kazami and the others, that time had arrived.

Rei closed her eyes to think.

The deeper they dove into the dungeon, the stronger the monsters became. Every monster on the bottom floor was over level 1,000, and they often encountered ten or more of them at once. She doubted she could manage on her own before support appeared.

Her only option was to enter the boss room with Kazami's party.

"Fine. I'll go with you."

"Wonderful! I knew you'd understand!" Kazami gave a truly plastic smile.

Then, he opened the door to the boss room. They stepped boldly inside—except Rei, who followed last, her courage barely intact.

The door slowly closed behind them. Rei turned around; seeing it shut made her realize something else important. She couldn't hope for reinforcements anymore.

The next time that door opened, she feared their whole party would be dead.

Rei and the others gazed up at the final boss towering before them.

The high orc was a *lot* larger than last time. At three hundred and ten centimeters tall, it had grown nearly a meter in size. Rock-hard muscles bulged across its body, and it carried its heavy iron axe with ease. Its power was clearly immense.

"Well, this is a surprise. It *does* look strong. Sakura, can you use Appraisal on it?" Kazami asked.

"Only on the level. This high orc is level 3,000!"

Hearing the number made them tense. Kazami was only level 2,300, and he was the highest leveled among them. Against such an overwhelming enemy, all of them were afraid. All except for Kazami.

"Ha ha ha! This is fantastic! Think of the glory we'll get from victory over *that*!" he exclaimed. "No reason to fear, everyone! We've defeated every strong opponent that came our way. Trust yourselves!"

The words resonated with Sakura and the others. Their expressions hardened.

"You're right," she answered. "We've overcome scores of strong enemies just like this one!"

"That's it, get fired up!"

"We'll crush it!"

Unlike her excited teammates, Rei and her mere level of 600 could only stand back and watch the Kings of Unique face off with the high orc. No matter who won, it would be a fight to the death.

Ten minutes into the battle, Rei's party had every reason to celebrate. They had the upper hand.

"Ha! You call this level 3,000? Lightning Strike!"

The powerful strike halted the high orc's movements and made it roar in pain.

"Now, everyone!"

A massive explosion burst, with the high orc as the epicenter. When the smoke cleared, their enemy stood in tatters.

The high orc was *level 3,000.* At first, Rei didn't know what would happen, but the unique skills the party possessed made up for the level difference and then some. The advantage was with them from the start.

I never expected they could overpower the high orc so drastically.

Watching them from behind, Rei couldn't help but be impressed. Unique skills were honestly invaluable.

"Yuuya! Trap it while you can!" Kazami ordered.

"Got it... Fortress: Seal!"

Dozens of pillars shot from the ground and trapped the high orc inside a prison, halting its movements. Kazami nodded with satisfaction.

"We're safe now. All we have to do is wail on it until it dies. It was less of a challenge than I expected, but whatever. C'mon, let's wrap this up."

Kazami stood in front of the imprisoned high orc and raised his hands. Rei suspected, as she was sure the others did, that he could win with a full-powered lightning strike.

Suddenly, the high orc let out an earsplitting roar. The boss room shuddered.

What in the world? A sense of foreboding shuddered through Rei's body. The others ignored it, and an annoyed expression crossed Kazami's face.

"*That's* your last-ditch move? Pathetic!" he said. "Sucks for you, but I'm going to kill...you..."

He trailed off in disbelief at the sight before him. Something began to rise from the boss room floor—creatures clad in silver armor with longswords in their hands. Five of them in total emerged, as if one was meant for each party member.

Kazami shouted, unable to hide the shock in his voice. "Sakura! What the heck are those things?!"

"I'm using Appraisal now! They're called Nameless Knights, and they're each level 2,000!"

"More enemies?! No one said anything about the final boss having minions! But if they're that low-level... *Lightning Strike!!!*"

Lightning flashed from Kazami's fingers and struck the five knights. But the knights kept stalking toward them, as if they hadn't taken damage at all.

"One strike won't kill them…? That's a lot of defense, but how many hits can they take? Yuuya! Kousuke! Hold them back for me!!!"

If their resident tank and swordsman drew the monsters' attention, he could strike them down. At least, they assumed it would work, until the knights unexpectedly moved toward *him*.

"Hey, how are they smart enough to target the sorcerer?! Dammit!"

The knights advanced upon him. Until now, he'd defeated monsters from a distance. This was the first time that Kazami had to rely on Yuuya and Kousuke to defend him at close range. That was precisely why he mistimed his evasive maneuver.

A knight's sword descended upon Kazami.

"Magic Sword!"

Rei activated her unique skill. Aware she couldn't defeat the knight herself, she used her wind blade to snag the knight's footsteps. The knight stumbled, and the sword barely grazed the end of Kazami's nose.

"Don't underestimate me! Lightning Strike!"

Kazami directed a rage-fueled attack at the enemy that wounded him, eliminating it in a flash of light.

"Ha! See that? That's what happens to weaklings who get a big head!" he shouted smugly. He didn't even thank Rei before he turned to his next target.

Rei clutched her chest above her pounding heart and breathed a sigh of relief.

I'm glad I acted in time.

Despite the sudden change in the odds, the party defeated each knight one by one, until only one remained.

"One more to go!" Kazami said. "Let's knock it on its butt and finish off the high—"

Suddenly, the room jolted and roiled with the force of an earthquake.

"What's going on?!" Kazami shouted.

"I don't know! Definitely nothing good," Sakura said. "Let's defeat the high orc quickly and get out of..."

Sakura lost her words, her face a mixture of shock, fear, and disbelief. Rei and Kazami followed her gaze to the high orc and immediately understood.

"No way... It broke the prison," Rei gasped.

"There's more! The wounds we inflicted are healed, and it's *growing*!"

It was supposed to be trapped. While they were battling the Nameless Knights, the high orc had destroyed the prison and freed itself. Now, it towered menacingly at over four meters tall. Not to mention it was back to *full health*.

None of the five party members could explain the high orc's

transformation, but the goosebump-inducing intimidation it radiated was undeniable.

"This is a joke. What is *happening*?"

"Is it just me or is that thing *way* more powerful?"

"This isn't possible..."

The other party members were convinced there was some kind of mistake. Rei trembled where she stood, unable to bring herself to help them. Beneath her fear, she grappled with the situation.

If a dungeon collapse powers up the boss monster, that means we entered this room before that power up was complete. While we were fighting the knights, the high orc grew stronger still...

Now, there was nothing they could do about it.

Rei worked up the courage to ask Sakura, "What is the high orc's level?"

Sakura's answer revealed how out of their depths they were.

"That isn't a high orc anymore." Her voice shook as she spoke. "It evolved into an orc general...and it's level 4,000."

In other words: this beast became their death sentence.

The emergence of the orc general more than turned the tide of the battle against their party, it slammed the tide into them like a tsunami. Kazami faced the orc general and shot Lightning Strike after Lightning Strike, but it didn't stop moving toward him.

"No, no, *no*! Why won't it work? Why won't my lightning inflict any damage?!"

This was the first time Kazami had faced an enemy that didn't succumb to his attacks, and it made him visibly panic. Technically speaking, he *was* doing damage, but in his frazzled state, he couldn't see he was lowering its HP.

Kazami wasn't the only one in a downward spiral. With their unique skills rendered useless, Sakura and the others gradually lost the will to fight. As the lowest leveled, Rei could only watch helplessly. She'd get in the way if she attacked.

I didn't realize this party was so fragile.

They had leaned on their unique skills, so much so they convinced themselves they were equal to superior opponents. But they were wrong.

Defeating higher level opponents before didn't make them superior. They were nothing more than low-rank adventurers who relied on their skills to win. The orc general was the first opponent to challenge them beyond that.

What did they know about fighting their way out of a real threat? The Kings of Unique had never fought with the cold blade of a knife against their throat. Facing a true threat, they swayed on the precipice of death. In a matter of moments, they'd slip off the edge.

Like the knight, the orc general suddenly turned toward Kazami.

"How—"

Kazami froze before his enemy's powerful form.

"Watch out!" Rei shouted.

"Rei?!"

She ran into the fray, unable to stand back and watch.

Her Magic Sword couldn't do anything to that monster's giant body, but she managed to push Kazami down before the iron axe fell. The axe slammed on the ground beside her. The shockwave alone forced the breath from her lungs and sent her flying. Chunks of the broken ground sprayed over her. She rolled until she struck the boss room's wall.

Huh? I can't...move...

Her body wouldn't listen to her mind's pleas. She could barely lift a finger. The world around her became veiled in red, as if she was bleeding from somewhere. A warning signal flashed in her vision and indicated that a small fraction of her HP remained. It dwindled with every second.

She willed herself to watch the battle through her blurred vision.

It was nearing its end.

The orc general thundered a war cry that violently shook the room. It lifted the iron axe with both hands, as if it wasn't satisfied with one.

What's it doing?

It didn't move like before, when it wanted to strike Kazami quickly. Rei realized it was bracing itself to hit with maximum destructive power, but she couldn't muster the strength to shout a warning. She hovered like a ghost on the sidelines, barely conscious.

"Wh-what is it doing?"

"St-stop!"

"This can't be happening..."

Sakura, Yuuya, and Kousuke watched on in horror and confusion. Kazami stood before the orc general, lifted his hands stiffly to hide his trembling, and shouted as loudly as he could.

"As if *I'd* die here! Lightning Strike!"

His lightning flashed white, brighter than she'd seen before. He'd poured his heart into the strongest attack he'd ever unleashed.

But even as the lightning struck the orc general, it howled. The axe swung down and cut through the blast. It created an ear-splitting boom as it smashed the ground.

Explosive. Violent.

Those words were insufficient to express the sonic boom that struck the entire party. Debris burst in every direction. The ground hollowed out, and the orc general vanished into the cloud of rubble.

What's happening...?

Since she'd already flown into a corner of the room, the fragments didn't reach Rei, but the same couldn't be said for the others. A few seconds later, the dust cleared and she saw the aftermath.

"N-no..."

The fragments and the resulting shock wave hit the others at point-blank range. Now, they lay scattered across the room, unconscious, barely breathing. They'd sustained severe injuries.

If left untreated, they would most certainly die. Even if the attack had left them unscathed, they couldn't beat the orc general.

The result of this battle would be defeat.

The orc general regarded them sprawled on the ground, turned its back on them, and walked away—almost as if their puny existences weren't worth its time. Especially Rei, who was low level but in better shape than the others. At least, until her HP depleted entirely.

A lesser creature didn't want to allow even that to play out. A knight lurking since the awakening of the orc general rose, a longsword in its hands. It walked slowly toward Rei.

Once it finished her off, it would turn its blade on the others. She desperately tried to get up, but her body was helpless.

This is where I die.

Achingly, Rei moved her eyes to the door of the boss room. It remained tightly shut with no sign of opening.

Obviously—that was how dungeons worked. No one could open that door and come to their rescue. It would be a miracle, and heroes only existed in fiction. Too bad it took so long for her to realize that.

Where had she gone wrong? Was it when she joined the Kings of Unique? When she failed to stop Kazami and the others from facing the boss? When she entered the boss room with them? No clear answer came to her, but such was life. Everything had to end, so there was no point questioning it. Still, that was *why* her defiant heart questioned it.

Couldn't something different have happened?

At least no one else would die from their foolish choice. Once they succumbed to death, the door would open and the B-rank party would enter and defeat the orc general. That was the best she could hope for.

The Nameless Knight raised its longsword. Rei quietly closed her eyes.

Thud.

It sounded like something hard fell on the ground.

Why...doesn't it hurt? She'd heard the sound, but pain didn't follow. Full of fear, Rei opened her eyes.

"Sorry, I'm late."

That voice. That broad back.

"How...?"

She couldn't believe who was in front of her. It wasn't possible for him to be *in* here.

The knight's helmet rolled on the ground. The body collapsed with a loud clang. Rei knew the man who had beheaded the knight with his silver longsword.

Amane Rin.

One hour after the Kings of Unique stormed Kenzaki Dungeon.

After discussing their progress with other adventurers, Rin confirmed they'd successfully cleared out the monsters that had surfaced. That done, he and Yui made tracks for Kenzaki.

"Yui, how's your strength holding up? You've stuck with me this whole time."

"I'm good! I'm an adventurer too, you know!"

She didn't seem to be putting on a brave face. In fact, she practically bubbled with energy.

She's something else.

He was a little surprised to see Yui so perky. In just one hour, she had healed nearly twenty injured people. She'd drunk mana recovery potions to keep her MP up, but even with that in mind, Yui had accomplished more than he expected from her level. Her talent for healing might exceed the high potential he estimated earlier.

When they reached Kenzaki, they found a crowd of adventurers on standby near the entrance. Two adventurers with the same emblem—a moon and a sword—on their armor made Rin suspect they were there to defeat the final boss.

Based on that emblem, they belonged to the Yoizuki Guild: the very guild Yui and Rin had talked about. Then again, it wasn't unusual to see them since Yoizuki Headquarters was located nearby. In their hands, the final boss was bound for a beating.

They didn't look as relieved as Rin felt. The same could be said for the adventurers around them; there was a restlessness he couldn't pin down. He approached a man from the Yoizuki Guild.

"Excuse me, but did something go wrong? Everyone seems worried."

"The thing is..."

The man explained everything: the Kings of Unique arrived shortly before the Yoizuki Guild and offered to clear the path to the boss room. Twenty minutes later, the Yoizuki Guild's B-rank team of six went in after them. The two members on the surface stayed as points of contact and as a preventative measure in case the final boss rose to the surface. They were supposed to regroup with the Kings of Unique and work together to defeat the final boss. Everything was according to plan—until one of Yoizuki's members used their Telepathy skill to notify them that the boss room door wouldn't open.

The Kings of Unique were already inside.

Over ten minutes had passed since then.

"*What*?!" Rin exclaimed. He couldn't help himself. That meant Kazami and the rest of his party were fighting the final boss *as they spoke*.

He had no idea how Kazami became responsible for clearing the way, but despite only knowing him for a short time, he knew Kazami's motivation. In the pursuit of fame, he must have chosen to endanger the party and challenge the final boss.

Okay, it was a foolish choice, but it's too early to write them off, he told himself. Their group was over level 2,000, and with their unique skills, they were strong.

"Wait. Where's Rei?" he wondered aloud.

Fear raced up his spine as he remembered her. She was the only under-leveled member of the Kings of Unique.

A nearby adventurer overheard Rin and said, "I don't know who that 'Rei' girl is, but I saw five of them go in."

That spiked Rin's panic much higher. If Kazami planned to lead them to the final boss from the start, would Rei have knowingly gone with them?

No, she would not. They'd dived together, so he knew she wasn't the type to make reckless moves, which meant Kazami didn't just fool the people here. He fooled *Rei*, his own party member, into thinking they wouldn't try it alone.

Heck, if Rei had stayed behind, it would've been *better* for their odds. Kazami schemed his way into this mess without thinking at all!

Rin felt like restless, cornered prey. It only worsened when a violent tremor erupted from deep within the dungeon. The two Yoizuki Guild members started at the same time.

"What the?!"

"Ahh!"

"Not good! The dungeon collapse has entered the final stages. We're out of time!"

"The boss is going to emerge. We need to buy time to stop it."

"Not just that. The more the dungeon collapses, the stronger the final boss gets. That tremor probably meant the boss is alive in the boss room but even stronger. And the people fighting it..."

Rin's heart nearly leapt out of his chest. He knew exactly what words finished that sentence. Kazami's party had been fighting the final boss for ten minutes. If they hadn't defeated it in that time and it was even stronger now, their odds of defeating it were zero.

Rei and the others were on the brink of death. He couldn't stand by and wait any longer.

"I'll be back," he told Yui.

"Rin-senpai, what are you talking—Rin?!"

He sprinted toward the entrance to the Return Zone. If he had activated Dungeon Teleportation while standing in the crowd, he might make it inside undetected. It'd be a different story when he returned via the dungeon's teleportation magic. If he didn't enter through the Gate, he'd definitely draw suspicion.

As he ran, the man from Yoizuki called after him. "Hold it! What do you think you're—"

Close enough to the gate that it wouldn't be strange if he disappeared, Rin whispered his skill command.

"Dungeon Teleportation."

He activated his skill again and again in quick succession, rapidly dropping through the floors. Rin prayed his gut feeling was wrong, that Kazami's party had the chops to win against a beefed-up final boss. Best case scenario, he'd use Evasion to erase his presence, then activate Dungeon Teleportation to escape.

He'd get yelled at for charging into the dungeon without permission, but he could write it off later as puberty or something. He *prayed* this would end that uneventfully. But reality wasn't so kind.

When he teleported into the boss room, he arrived in a disaster zone.

Most of the Kings of Unique lay wounded and unconscious. Only Rei clung to consciousness, but a Nameless Knight was poised to strike her down. At least no one was dead. Their lives could still be saved.

Rin summoned Nameless from his Item Box and brought the blade down hard, severing the knight's head.

"Sorry I'm late," he told Rei.

"H-how...?" she gasped. She was covered in blood, so weak she could hardly talk.

This is bad, Rin thought. He withdrew a high-level HP recovery potion from his Item Box and helped her slowly drink it. With the high profits of the past week, he'd stocked up. In this moment, he was relieved he bought them.

"One of these will fully restore HP for anyone under level 1,000. You're safe now."

"R-Rin," she coughed. "How did you get in here?"

"I'll answer later. We've got other things to take care of. Once you can move, give these potions to the others." Rin handed four more healing potions to her, then rose to face the dungeon's master.

The orc general had noticed Rin's sudden arrival and picked him as the next victim of its massacre. It lifted the iron axe and stepped into a stance that indicated it could dash toward him at any moment.

Rin calmly used Appraisal on his powerful opponent.

"Final boss, orc general. Level 4,000? Yikes. Makes me want to get the heck out of here..."

But he didn't run. This was like his fight against the Nameless Knight. If he was the type to run in the face of a stronger enemy, he wouldn't have walked this path.

He gripped his special silver longsword and faced off against the orc general.

"You haven't shown me your true worth since we fought the knight, eh, Nameless?"

Not a single tremor of fear moved through his body as he focused on the enemy in front of him.

"Here we go, orc general. I'll show you how weaklings *fight*."

With a determined step forward, he dove into battle.

AMANE RIN

LEVEL: 2,773   **SP:** 210

TITLES: Dungeon Traveler (4/10), Nameless Swordsman

HP: 22,200/22,200   **MP:** 5,350/5,530

ATTACK: 5,610   **DEFENSE:** 4,430   **SPEED:** 5,950

INTELLIGENCE: 3,850   **RESISTANCE:** 4,130   **LUCK:** 3,760

SKILLS: Dungeon Teleportation LV 12, Enhanced Strength LV MAX, Herculean Strength LV MAX, Superhuman Strength LV 3, High-speed Movement LV MAX, Gale Wind LV 3, Mana Boost LV 2, Mana Recovery LV 2, Enemy Detection LV 4, Evasion LV 4, Status Condition Resistance LV 4, Appraisal, Item Box LV 5

ENHANCED STRENGTH LV MAX: +100 to Attack, Defense, and Speed

HERCULEAN STRENGTH LV MAX: +3,000 Attack

HIGH-SPEED MOVEMENT LV MAX: +3,000 Speed

MANA BOOST LV 2: +20% to MP

MANA RECOVERY LV 2: +20% to MP recovery

SWORD OF THE NAMELESS KNIGHT

A sword used by the Nameless Knight,

RECOMMENDED EQUIP LEVEL: 2,000

ATTACK +2,000

When an enemy (human or monster) is of a higher level than the wielder, all parameters except HP and MP increase by 30% each.

CHAPTER 8

WHAT IT MEANS TO BE WEAK

AMANE RIN's fight to the death with the orc general was fierce from the start. Nameless and the iron axe clashed together in a swordfight that echoed off the boss room's walls. Their blades etched a flurry of slashes and arcs in the air.

Rin swung his blade in an unusual way. He made shallow cut after shallow cut in the orc general's body. Conversely, the orc general executed heavy, final blows. Here and there, Nameless deflected the axe. The orc never landed the finisher that it aimed for.

Rin wasn't winning by any means. In fact, he was on the razor-thin edge of losing. One solid hit would take him down, but one strike from him barely made a scratch. It was an unequal match.

This isn't good, but I have to carry on.

Each dodge wore away at Rin's nerves, but he had no other options. This was the only way he could fight. Sure, the orc general *could* deliver massive damage in one strike but fighting agilely created openings. He prioritized dodging his enemy's attacks above all else.

Attack and evade: that was how Rin had survived for that long.

Hopeless as this situation was, he powered through it. Enemy territory or not, he didn't relent. He pursued his opponent with his speed-based fighting style, but would his efforts bear fruit?

Slowly, gradually, Rin's strikes multiplied as he worked to outmaneuver the orc general.

Rei carefully dosed the other party members with potions and retreated to a location where she wouldn't get in the way of the fight.

As she watched Rin fight the orc general, she whispered a soft "Wow..."

He didn't hesitate in the face of an overwhelming enemy, just like the heroes she admired in her stories. Every time he swung his sword, her heart beat faster and faster.

"But how is he doing it?"

As uplifted and inspired as she felt, she had *big* questions that needed answering. How did Rin pass the closed boss room door? How had he gained such an immense power boost—enough to fight on par with an orc general—after one week?

I remember.

Months ago, Kazami mentioned a former member of the Kings of Unique, someone who'd held them back. Amane Rin, bearer of a unique skill called Dungeon Teleportation, which turned out to be useless.

"Dungeon...*Teleportation*."

In that moment, she understood how he got inside. It was right there in the name of his skill. If he could freely move within a dungeon, a locked door was no obstacle.

But that left one more mystery: a week ago, when they traveled Kenzaki Dungeon together, he was around level 1,000 or so. Someone in that level range couldn't clash head-to-head with a level 4,000 orc general and stay standing. It made no sense. No matter how many level-up rewards he gained, which dungeon gave them to him, or how many monsters he defeated for experience points, it wasn't possible to grow that much in a short amount of time.

So, how had he done it anyway?

"Oh!" His words from earlier popped into her mind.

I fulfilled my Dungeon Trav—ahem. *I beat a dungeon yesterday, so I'm taking the day to recharge.*

That was what he said, word-for-word. Kurosaki Rei was positive. Those words, alongside the fact he was here now, implied something incredible.

The puzzle pieces slotted together in her mind. The complete picture was an outlandish, ridiculous one, but if her hunch was correct, Rin was hiding an ability that could make him stronger than anyone else in the world.

"Is that really possible...?" she asked, but no one answered. She would only receive an answer if Rin defeated the orc general, and she survived to ask.

"Go win...Rin."

Rei clasped her hands together and prayed for his success.

As she watched, she realized she held one final question. Rin's attacks connected with the orc general, and he dodged every return strike from the terrible beast, yet the battle hadn't turned in his favor. He'd delivered countless blows, but none of them defeated it. The difference between him and the enemy was spread out before them like a vast and deep ocean.

How did he fight on without drowning in despair?

Against such a powerful enemy, she, Kazami, and the rest of their party lost hope. But Rin possessed something unyielding within him: something the rest of them were missing.

Amane Rin knew he was weak. That was why he could fight enemies that were stronger than him.

On the battlefield, unnecessary emotions would hold him back. Pride, rashness, and even fear were all useless in the wake of battle. So he cut himself off from those feelings. Instead, he focused on the enemy in front of him, hoping to seize the thin, fluttering thread of victory.

Weak people put everything on the line to win. A strong enemy should fear a weak opponent in that mental state.

Eventually, Rin was the only one swinging his weapon. The orc general roared and leapt back. It must have known it was losing leverage.

"You won't get away from me!"

Rin charged forward in pursuit of the orc general. He couldn't afford to yield even a centimeter. The orc general chopped the iron axe in a wide arc, not vertically this time but horizontally, slicing into the ground. The ground shattered and pelted Rin with fragments of dirt. No matter how many he parried, more followed. He dodged and dodged, which only served to slow him down.

Not so fast!

"Enemy Detection."

The skill activated. He usually used it to detect the mana—and therefore the locations—of nearby people or monsters, but as pieces of the dungeon itself, the fragments held mana too. Thanks to the skill, he deciphered the trajectory of incoming debris and pursued the orc general without lowering his speed.

Rin's quick thinking helped him catch the orc general unprepared to parry. The odds that he could land a hit with his full strength behind it soared. Without hesitation, he stepped into stance.

"Rin, watch out!" Rei called somewhere behind him.

He saw why she yelled. The orc general was making an unprecedented move. It cast the iron axe aside and clapped its tremendous hands together. The absence of the weapon cost the orc general power, but it boosted speed—fast enough to raise its fists over Rin, ready to crush him.

There was no time to dodge, but if he stayed still and countered with his sword, he'd meet a tragic end all the same.

"Sorry, but I'm not new to fighting this way," he muttered.

Then he moved *faster*.

The orc general's giant fists passed through empty air and smashed the ground where he had stood. He hurtled forward as if wind pushed at his back.

> **Gale Wind LV 3: +30% to speed (COSTS 10 MP PER SECOND)**

Gale Wind unlocked when High-speed Movement was maxed out. He'd obtained the skill yesterday, but since the MP cost was so high, he'd waited to use it. With victory within his grasp, he didn't hesitate to activate it and use the extra boost to evade the orc general's attack.

Was it *too* much of a speed boost? In an instant, he ended up closer to the orc general than he intended. He was in no position to properly swing his sword, but that didn't stop him. If the orc general wanted to play dirty and fight with its bare hands, so would he.

"Payback time!"

With his weapon now stored in his Item Box, he punched the orc general with a full-powered, *satisfying* uppercut. The orc general staggered backwards.

Alongside Gale Wind, he'd activated a skill he unlocked once he maxed out Herculean Strength: *Superhuman* Strength.

> **Superhuman Strength LV 3: +30% to attack (COSTS 10 MP PER SECOND)**

"Here comes the final blow!"

He kept Gale Wind and Superhuman Strength active while he summoned Nameless from his Item Box once more. His MP was burning away to nothing, but sacrifices had to be made. Gut instinct told him the fight's finale was imminent.

He prepared for one final, fierce attack.

With the orc general off balance, he danced around its body with rapid speed and slashed repeatedly at its arms, legs, and torso. Everywhere was wide open. Gashes opened up across the orc general.

Final stretch. Amane Rin was sure of it.

Defenseless and too injured to attack, the orc general bellowed with all its might, which released a strong gust in his direction. It knocked him off-balance, but he forced himself steady. The orc general grasped the iron axe and released one more long war cry. Its muscles bulged, and it seemed satisfied as its eyes glowed red. It would soon attempt a counterattack.

That was the orc general's biggest mistake.

"Raaaaargh!!!"

One second, Rin was there. The next second, he wasn't.

The orc had wasted the time Rin needed to activate the very skill that made their fight possible. He couldn't know it, but his move paralleled the trick the orc general had used to get the time to power itself up against Kazami's party. With a distraction, he had created an opening.

◆⟱◆

The orc general didn't, but Rei saw where Rin went. After he whispered the command under his breath, he'd vanished—until he appeared in the air above the orc general's head.

"I knew it. *That's* what he's doing."

Rei felt her theory becoming fact as Rin kicked off the ceiling and rocketed toward the orc general. Gravity turned him into an arrow, with Nameless as the arrowhead.

The orc general realized where Rin was and roared as it made a desperate swing of the iron axe.

"Nice try!" Rin shouted. A last-ditch attack like that couldn't break him.

He spun past the iron axe in mid-air and channeled the energy into his attack. The climax was upon them.

"You're *finiiiiiished*!"

Amane Rin poured every ounce of his ability into his blade. It shone white and carved a crescent moon of brilliant light in the air as he sliced. He landed with a thud on one knee. A moment later, the orc general's head slid from its neck and rolled across the ground, away from its collapsing body.

Rin rose and flicked Nameless a few times to get the blood off.

"It's over, Rei," he said, turning to her with a reassuring smile.

The system dinged in my mind.

"*You have defeated the final boss.*"

"*Gained XP: Level increased by 233!*"

"Final boss takedown reward: Level increased by 150."

"Title: 'Endbringer (ERROR)' unlocked."

Whoa, that was a treasure trove of experience points, probably because the orc general was level 4,000. One battle, and I'd gained nearly four hundred levels! The new title would have to wait. First and foremost, I had some things to take care of.

I turned to Rei, the only other adventurer nearby. Her eyes shimmered as she smiled.

"Rin... Thank you for saving us."

"Of course. I'm glad everyone's safe."

From the looks of it, they were all alive. Relief washed over me as I really realized I had saved everyone.

Rei told me the story of what happened. I imagined most of it correctly, with Kazami's egotistical decision at the heart of it all.

"It's good that no one died, but he still endangered other people. We need to make sure he takes a long hard look at himself in the mirror after this," I said.

"The rest of us need to reflect on our actions too. We failed to stop him," she said heavily.

"Rei... Don't say that."

Seeing Rei so woebegone, I patted her on the head. She looked up at me with a strange expression, but she didn't object.

Admittedly, I couldn't argue with her basic premise. She and the rest of her party bore some responsibility for what happened, but for now, no one would punish her for feeling relief.

"Let yourself enjoy being alive. You're here to tell the tale, right?"

"Right. When you put it like that, I will." She grinned, until she jumped as if remembering something. "Now, *you* tell *me* what happened! How did you get here? The boss room door was closed."

"Uh, about that..."

I debated how much I should explain, exactly, but she answered for me.

"Was it Dungeon Teleportation?"

"You knew about it?" Hearing those words out of her mouth surprised me, but Kazami *had* told her about me. It made sense he'd also told her about my unique skill. It wasn't that problematic if she knew I'd used it to get past the sealed door.

If only that was where her questions stopped.

"Does Dungeon Teleportation allow you to bypass a Span too?"

"It...does not."

"Oh. So it does," she said with certainty.

"I just said it doesn't!" I shouted back without thinking, but Rei just gave me a small smile.

"Don't worry, I won't tell anyone. If people found out you grew *this* strong in such a short amount of time, you'd definitely run into trouble."

Yeah, it didn't seem like I could fool her. I was the one who let it slip that I was under a Span and then ran in here. It would've been a matter of time before she put the clues together. I was grateful she didn't dig for the truth in earshot of anyone else.

"Thanks for your concern," I said. "I'd appreciate it if you kept it between us."

"I wouldn't betray the man who saved my life."

"I believe you."

"Good." I had no choice but to trust her. Besides, she didn't strike me as the type to break promises.

That out of the way, we had a different problem to solve.

"We still need to figure out what we say once the dungeon teleportation magic kicks in and we return to the surface," I said. "How should we explain who defeated the final boss?"

"Can't you use your skill to exit the boss room and head back up by yourself?"

I shook my head. "That's not what I mean. Once the final boss is gone, the dungeon collapse destroys the Return Zone too. Everyone inside the dungeon will appear at the same time, including anyone outside the boss room. I think that'll make it easy to hide where I've been, but we need to come up with an explanation for how the boss went down. Everyone's unconscious except for you."

"You're right. That *does* seem fishy—oh!" Rei's pitch heightened as an idea struck her. "How about this? Just before everyone blacked out, Kazami-san unleashed a full-powered Lightning Strike that triggered an explosion when it struck the orc general. The explosion enveloped everyone and knocked them out, but it took down the orc general in the process."

"That would make everyone's unconscious state work in our favor, but is it convincing enough?"

"I wouldn't mind saying I landed the final blow, but Kazami and the others know that my injuries were so bad, I couldn't lift a finger. I doubt that would add any believability."

"I guess it'll have to do as is. Though, when Kazami wakes up and hears what he supposedly accomplished, won't he get a big head about it?" I'd rather not pin the success on Kazami's party, however strangely obtained, if it meant he pulled another stunt like this.

"I think it'll be okay. This incident taught us a lesson about the dangers of dungeons. If it ever happens again, I'll act responsibly and stop everyone before it gets to this point."

Rei's resolute face erased my doubt. "Okay. Let's go with that story," I replied.

"Got it."

One thing left to do.

"We'd better collect the spoils," I said.

When I first arrived, it was a Nameless Knight preparing to attack Rei. I was unlikely to snag another Nameless in the future, so I checked our surroundings. Sadly, I couldn't find it anywhere.

"Rin? What's the matter?" Rei asked.

"I don't see the Nameless Knight's corpse."

"It vanished while you were fighting the orc general."

"Aww, really?"

The way Rei explained their encounter, it sounded like the Nameless Knights spawned in irregular patterns. The irregular boss and unusually fast collapse probably impacted that.

"Better harvest this, at least," I said.

I extracted the magic stone from the orc general's body. I'd never seen one so pure and clear before. This thing must be worth millions of yen. I was the one who really defeated it, so there was no harm in taking it, right?

A soft light enveloped me, Rei, and the unconscious members of the Kings of Unique.

"Right on time," I said.

The teleportation spell was about to send us to the Return Zone. In the short time it took to activate, Rei asked me, "How are *you* going to explain away rushing into the dungeon?"

"I forgot about that. Uh, blame it on puberty or something?"

She cocked her head at me questioningly.

Please, Rei, don't look at me like I'm an idiot.

Finally, the spell's effects activated, and with the final boss defeated, we returned to the surface.

AMANE RIN

LEVEL: 3,156   **SP:** 4,010

TITLES: Dungeon Traveler (4/10), Nameless Swordsman, Endbringer (Error)

HP: 25,280/25,280   **MP:** 1,930/6,280

ATTACK: 6,410   **DEFENSE:** 5,000   **SPEED:** 6,870

INTELLIGENCE: 4,350   **RESISTANCE:** 4,670   **LUCK:** 4,260

SKILLS: Dungeon Teleportation LV 12, Enhanced Strength LV MAX, Herculean Strength LV MAX, Superhuman Strength LV 3, High-speed Movement LV MAX, Gale Wind LV 3, Mana Boost LV 2, Mana Recovery LV 2, Enemy Detection LV 4, Evasion LV 4, Status Condition Resistance LV 4, Appraisal, Item Box LV 5

ENDBRINGER (ERROR)

A title given to someone who defeats a final boss solo.

Grants +30% to all status parameters except HP during combat
  against a final boss.

ERROR: Unfulfilled condition detected. Until this condition is
  fulfilled, this title's effects cannot be displayed.

EPILOGUE

EVERYTHING WENT SMOOTHLY after I defeated the orc general—ha! As if.

The second we materialized, the dungeon supervisor and the Yoizuki Guild members gave us the lecture of a lifetime. Rei, for challenging the final boss without waiting for backup. Me, for charging into the dungeon during a collapse.

Puberty didn't cut it as an excuse, as it turned out.

Rei conveyed the supposed details for how the final boss came down. Kazami's do-or-die attack was the final blow. Coming from her, everyone accepted the events. There was no point in her lying, and technically, Kazami *had* landed the last blow. Before I came along, at least.

Once the Kings of Unique regained consciousness, they'd be questioned to corroborate Rei's story. They wouldn't remember anything that happened after they passed out, so they'd have to take her word for it. It would work itself out.

That was all the explanation we had to offer, so the interrogation ended there. They nearly forced me to wait for Kazami and the others to wake up and respond to questioning, but after what we'd been through, they allowed us to leave.

Rei, Yui, and I began the walk toward the station.

Yui broke the silence. "You surprised me by leaping into the dungeon like that. You were so desperate you forgot the boss room door wouldn't open for you!"

"Yeah, exactly. Embarrassing, isn't it?" I replied, nodding along.

Good thing Yui got the wrong idea, or I would have more excuses to make. She could keep her misunderstanding.

"It wasn't like that," Rei said.

"Rei?"

She grabbed onto my opposite arm and said with a kind, steadying voice, "He didn't do anything *embarrassing*. He came to save me, which I was very grateful for... Um, not that it worked, but still."

"*Rei.* You're killing me," I hissed. While I wanted to say something to save my dignity, I couldn't without admitting I teleported inside the boss room. My image was taking massive damage. On the other hand, Rei had made her feelings clear, and that was nice to hear.

"Is it just me or do you two suddenly seem closer?" Yui grumbled. "Take *this*!"

In a burst of movement, she grabbed my free arm and clutched it tight against her chest.

"Uh, Yui?" Did she pick something up from the conversation that I didn't?

Rei and Yui glared at each other with so much intensity that I could practically see sparks clashing between them.

"I *knew* it," Rei growled at her. "You too, huh?"

"I'm not going to lose, Rei-chan!"

I had no idea what got them on a first-name basis, but I doubted it was good. Also, the arm-grabbing was making it pretty hard to walk.

"Oh well," I sighed. The whole reason I was in this position was my choice to face the orc general and save Rei's party. I decided to humor them.

"Come on, let's keep up the pace," I said.

"Okay!" Yui replied enthusiastically.

"Yeah," Rei agreed with a nod.

We peacefully—albeit quietly—resumed our walk forward.

That night, after I filled up on the dinner Hana made, I sat in my bedroom with my stat screen open. My new title stared back at me. With everything I needed to discuss with Rei, there was no time to consider the details, but now...

"Endbringer, huh? That's a disturbing title."

A title given to someone who defeated a final boss solo *and* granted +30 percent to all status parameters except HP during combat against a final boss? It was a pretty sweet boost. The odd thing was the title's second feature.

"'*Error: Unfulfilled condition has been detected.*' This kind of makes sense, I think. I didn't inflict the damage entirely solo." Rei's party had damaged the orc general by the time I arrived. Bypassing the closed boss room door with Dungeon Teleportation must have created an irregularity.

"The effects only work if I'm fighting a final boss anyway, and that's hardly the next monster I'll see. Having a broken title shouldn't cause a problem."

I pushed the title to the back of my mind. Someday, I'd fulfill the conditions if the opportunity presented itself.

"I should focus on adding more dungeons to my Dungeon Traveler title." What would happen if I maxed it out with ten dungeons traveled to completion?

It was also about time I leveled up Dungeon Teleportation again. I was excited to see how my skill would evolve once it reached LV 20.

"I bet strengthening these will make me the strongest adventurer in the world one day."

The world's strongest adventurer. That goal was so high above my head, I could only just look up and see it—but that was temporary. Now I possessed the power to reach my goal.

I admired the strength of that adventurer who saved me, but the power destiny handed to me was a useless skill by the name of Dungeon Teleportation. Nevertheless, I didn't give up. I put in the blood, sweat, and tears. I *made* Dungeon Teleportation awaken into something more.

That power was in my hands. Starting today, I would use it to reach the top.

No, *not* starting today—in the year and a month since

starting as an adventurer, I'd believed that this power *would* become my future. I told myself what I'd known since my first day adventuring:

"I *will* become the best in the world...and I'll get there the fastest."

THE WORLD'S FASTEST
LEVEL▲UP

AT THE YOIZUKI GUILD

ONE WEEK AFTER *the dungeon collapse at Kenzaki Dungeon.*
The guild master of the Yoizuki Guild was alone at his desk when a rapid knock hammered on the door. He quickly assumed military-sharp posture.

"Come in," he said.

"Pardon my intrusion."

A beautiful young woman with long silver hair entered. His posture crumbled.

"Oh, it's you, Claire. I don't need to bother with appearances."

"Master, please. Pull yourself together or you'll set a bad example."

"Can't you be nicer and call me Papa?"

"Please let me draw a clear line between my private and public life. Besides, I wouldn't call you that even if decorum *did* allow for it, Master."

The guild master sulked. Claire didn't seem to pay him any mind.

"I've brought a report. I arrived late to the scene of Kenzaki's dungeon collapse, but the first party to descend successfully defeated it."

"Yes, I heard the gist of it. That first party had a rough time, but everything turned out all right. Good thing too."

"Certainly. The Kings of Unique were severely reprimanded for making the decision to engage the final boss on their own."

"Of course they were. One wrong move would've spelled disaster," he said. "*Wait.* Did you just say the 'Kings of Unique'?"

"You know of them?"

"Yes. They've made a name for themselves recently, but I've known about them for over a year. Although, didn't the collapse reach its final stages? Didn't think they had the strength to take down a final boss that powerful..."

"It was a narrow victory. Only one member remained conscious long enough to tell the full story."

Hearing that, the guild master leaned forward with interest. "I see. So the last member standing must've been Amane Rin... wait, no. I heard he left. Was it their leader, Kazami?"

"Negative. It was a recent recruit named Kurosaki Rei. She said Kazami landed the final blow—hold on. Did you say *Amane Rin*?"

"I did. Why do you ask?"

"Another person returned to the surface with the others. A solo adventurer who wasn't from the Kings of Unique *or* our guild. I'm positive his name was Amane Rin."

"What?" The guild master was on the edge of his seat. "He didn't help them defeat the final boss?"

"No. He stormed the dungeon *after* the Kings of Unique were battling the final boss. The door to the boss room wouldn't open for him, so he couldn't join the fight."

"That *would* be the logical conclusion."

The guild master was normally an optimistic and careless person, so when his expression turned serious, Claire was sure he had more to say.

"Do you know him?" she asked.

"Yes. I invited him to join our guild a year ago. He turned me down immediately, but I didn't have any business cards on me, so he might've thought I was a fraud."

"Master, if you invited him on the spot, was he *that* good?"

"Not particularly. He was weak, and everyone called him useless."

"Then why did you invite him?"

"His unique skill suggested a bright future, but what captured *my* interest were his eyes."

"His eyes, sir?" Claire tilted her head, puzzled.

The guild master nodded. "Right. He acted like a normal kid his age, but his eyes were different. They were narrow and focused, as if he had his eyes on a future where he reached his goals, whatever it took. They were a lot like yours."

"I see." Claire quietly closed her eyes, as if sinking into a memory.

"Anyway, thank you for the report. Let's be grateful this incident had no casualties," the guild master concluded.

"Indeed. I'll take my leave." Claire bowed, opened the door, and exited the guild master's office.

"Eyes like mine, huh?"

The eyes *she* remembered were of the deepest blue, like the sea.

Rin
Ar e

LEVEL

3156

SP 4010

STATUS

HP	25,280
MP	6,280
Attack	6,410
Defense	5,000
Speed	6,870
Intelligence	4,350
Resistance	4,670
Luck	4,260

SKILLS

Dungeon Teleportation LV 12
Enhanced Strength LV MAX
Herculean Strength LV MAX
Superhuman Strength LV 3
High-speed Movement LV MAX
Gale Wind LV 3
Mana Boost LV 2
Mana Recovery LV 2
Enemy Detection LV 4
Evasion LV 4
Status Condition Resistance LV 4
Appraisal
Item Box LV 5

ACHIEVEMENTS

Dungeon Traveler (4/10)
Nameless Swordsman
Endbringer (ERROR)

AFTERWORD

THANK YOU FOR PICKING UP a copy of *The World's Fastest Level Up*. I'm the author, Nagato Yamata.

I'm still not sure exactly what belongs in an afterword, but since I get one, I'll start with the origin behind this story. In recent years, I've been seeing the word "strong" pop up in popular light novels. Most of them showed a main character who was strong from start to finish. The word *strong* evokes feelings of security and exhilaration, so these stories were among my favorite reads. But in reading them, I came to a realization: I wanted to read a story about a character who starts out weak and *becomes* strong.

A character who works to grow is exciting: you never truly know if he can defeat every powerful enemy, building apprehension. Above all, imagine the *satisfaction* that comes from an underdog victory! Strong protagonists are great, don't get me wrong, but the appeal of a *growth*-oriented protagonist is what made me write *The World's Fastest Level Up*. I hope the engaging elements I wanted to include came to life for you in some way.

I originally released this story on a web novel platform, *Shousetsuka ni Narou*, or "Let's Be Novelists!", but when it was picked up for publication as a real book, I had to make huge revisions. Thanks to that, I think it's a lot closer to perfection compared to the web novel version. I intend to make large revisions for what will become Volume 2 as well. Not to mention, I think it'll be even more exciting than the first volume! I hope you look forward to it!

And I have some happy news to announce: *The World's Fastest Level Up* is getting a manga adaptation. Please keep an eye out for that version too!

Finally, I want to thank my managing editor S-san, fame-san for the beautiful illustrations, everyone who helped with advertising, and the many other people who helped bring this book into existence. Above all, I want to thank my readers from the bottom of my heart for giving this book a chance. I hope to see you in Volume 2.

—NAGATO YAMATA

FROM THE CREATORS

AUTHOR
NAGATO YAMATA

An Osaka resident, I currently write web novels. This is my first title with Kadokawa Sneaker Bunko. It's been a pleasure. I've always loved reading and writing about heroes doing cool things. This title is no exception. I hope you enjoy it!

ILLUSTRATOR
fame

Hello, fame here. This is the sixth light novel I've drawn illustrations for. All of them have been fantasy series, but this one feels fresh, since it overlays a contemporary setting. It's great to meet you!